LAST DUKE STANDING

(The Lords of Eton, Book 3)

As the third son of the Duke of Fordham, Alex never thought he'd become a duke. But he's suddenly catapulted to the lofty title after his slightly older brother dies in his sleep. Now Alex has the onerous task of announcing the death to the woman his brother was to wed.

Ever pragmatic, Lady Georgiana Fenton insists on seeing the late duke's body, and when she does, she's convinced he was smothered as he slept. She and the new duke decide to secretly work together to uncover the murderer. But the longer they're together, the harder it becomes to resist the duke's scorching kisses--and even harder to dismiss him from the list of suspects. No one had more to gain by her fiancé's death. . .

Some of the praise for Cheryl Bolen's writing:

"One of the best authors in the Regency romance field today." – *Huntress Reviews*

"Bolen's writing has a certain elegance that lends itself to the era and creates the perfect atmosphere for her enchanting romances." – *RT Book Reviews*

The Counterfeit Countess (Brazen Brides, Book 1)
Daphne du Maurier award finalist for Best Historical Mystery

"This story is full of romance and suspense. . . No one can resist a novel written by Cheryl Bolen. Her writing talents charm all readers. Highly recommended reading! 5 stars!" – *Huntress Reviews*

"Bolen pens a sparkling tale, and readers will adore her feisty heroine, the arrogant, honorable Warwick and a wonderful cast of supporting characters." – *RT Book Reviews*

His Golden Ring (Brazen Brides, Book 2)
"*Golden Ring*...has got to be the most PERFECT Regency Romance I've read this year." – *Huntress Reviews*

Holt Medallion winner for Best Historical, 2006

Lady By Chance (House of Haverstock, Book 1)
Cheryl Bolen has done it again with another sparkling Regency romance. . .Highly recommended – *Happily Ever After*

The Bride Wore Blue (Brides of Bath, Book 1)
Cheryl Bolen returns to the Regency England she knows so well. . .If you love a steamy Regency with a fast pace, be sure to pick up *The Bride Wore Blue*. – *Happily Ever After*

With His Ring (Brides of Bath, Book 2)
"Cheryl Bolen does it again! There is laughter, and the interaction of the characters pulls you right into the book. I look forward to the next in this series." – *RT Book Reviews*

The Bride's Secret (Brides of Bath, Book 3)
(originally titled *A Fallen Woman*)
"What we all want from a love story...Don't miss it!"
– *In Print*

To Take This Lord (Brides of Bath, Book 4)
(originally titled *An Improper Proposal*)
"Bolen does a wonderful job building simmering sexual tension between her opinionated, outspoken heroine and deliciously tortured, conflicted hero." – *Booklist of the American Library Association*

My Lord Wicked
Winner, International Digital Award for Best Historical Novel of 2011.

With His Lady's Assistance (Regent Mysteries, Book 1)
"A delightful Regency romance with a clever and personable heroine matched with a humble, but intelligent hero. The mystery is nicely done, the romance is enchanting and the secondary characters are enjoyable." – *RT Book Reviews*

Finalist for International Digital Award for Best Historical Novel of 2011.

A Duke Deceived
"*A Duke Deceived* is a gem. If you're a Georgette Heyer fan, if you enjoy the Regency period, if you like a genuinely sensuous love story, pick up this first novel by Cheryl Bolen."
– *Happily Ever After*

Books by Cheryl Bolen

Regency Romance

The Lords of Eton Series
The Portrait of Lady Wycliff (Book 1)
The Earl, the Vow, and the Plain Jane (Book 2)
Last Duke Standing (Book 3)

Brazen Brides Series
Counterfeit Countess (Book 1)
His Golden Ring (Book 2)
Oh What A (Wedding) Night (Book 3)
Miss Hastings' Excellent London Adventure
     (Book 4)
A Birmingham Family Christmas (Book 5)

House of Haverstock Series
Lady by Chance (Book 1)
Duchess by Mistake (Book2)
Countess by Coincidence (Book 3)
Ex-Spinster by Christmas (Book 4)

The Brides of Bath Series:
The Bride Wore Blue (Book 1)
With His Ring (Book 2)
The Bride's Secret (Book 3)
To Take This Lord (Book 4)
Love in the Library (Book 5)
A Christmas in Bath (Book 6)

Pride and Prejudice Sequels
Miss Darcy's New Companion
Miss Darcy's Secret Love
The Liberation of Miss de Bourgh

The Regent Mysteries Series:
   With His Lady's Assistance (Book 1)
   A Most Discreet Inquiry (Book 2)
   The Theft Before Christmas (Book 3)
   An Egyptian Affair (Book 4)

My Lord Wicked
A Duke Deceived

Novellas:
Christmas Brides (3 Regency Novellas)

Inspirational Regency Romance
Marriage of Inconvenience

Romantic Suspense
Texas Heroines in Peril Series:
   Protecting Britannia
   Capitol Offense
   A Cry in the Night
   Murder at Veranda House
Falling for Frederick

American Historical Romance
*A Summer to Remember (*3 American Historical Romances)

World War II Romance
It Had to be You

LAST DUKE STANDING

(The Lords of Eton, Book 3)

Cheryl Bolen

$\mathcal{C}$hapter 1

The calamitous intelligence that would redirect the course of Lord Alex Haversham's life was delivered to him while he sat in the library of his family's home. He and his boyhood friend Sinjin—Lord Slade—had come to Gosingham Hall not to partake of his ducal brother's shooting party but to draft penal reform legislation. Upon this frosty March morning, the members of the shooting party had departed while he and Sinjin debated the merits of transporting a man for depriving a hare of its life.

When the butler entered the chamber, Alex hardly looked up from the vellum upon which he was writing. Mannings cleared his throat and prefaced his remark with, "Your grace."

Had the servant's advanced years stolen away his faculties? Granted, Alex did vastly resemble his brother, the eighth Duke of Fordham, but Mannings had never in Alex's nine and twenty years confused the two siblings. Alex directed his attention to the butler.

Something was dreadfully wrong. Mannings' face had gone ashen, his hands trembled, and his voice quivered. "It's your brother."

Alex's heartbeat hammered. In the span of a second he linked *It's your brother* to the fact the butler had addressed him—the younger brother—as "your grace." *Dear Lord!* Freddie must be . . .

He eyed Mannings. "Dead?"

The butler nodded solemnly.

How could Freddie be gone? It hurt like the devil.

It was a moment before the new duke was cognizant enough to inquire about his brother's demise.

"Your brother has apparently died in his sleep, your grace."

Alex stood. "It can't be! I must see him."

"He's still in his bedchamber. A footman is staying with him."

"Has a surgeon been called?"

"I . . . I saw no need to send for one. The duke was clearly dead."

Alex nodded. He and Sinjin started up the broad staircase. As they approached the ducal bedchamber, Alex's gut clenched. His heartbeat roared. He did not want to step into the chamber. He wanted to open that door to a light-filled room where Freddie was strutting in front of a looking glass, admiring his well-tailored riding clothes and shiny boots. Of course, his cravat would have been tied to perfection, and nary a hair on his head would be out of place. Unlike Alex, Freddie had put great stock in appearances.

Alex froze. A feeling of agonizing grief flooded him. God, but he wished Freddie *would* be preening before that looking glass.

Sinjin patted him on the back. "I know this is going to be difficult. Allow me to go first." He opened the door.

Alex drew a deep breath and strode into the darkened chamber, fighting back tears. Even when he'd been on the battlefields in Spain surrounded by the stench of death—the deaths of young men under his command—he'd not cried. Crying was for women. He was determined not to let the tears spill now.

He saw the bed first. It was swathed in crimson silk, and a youthful footman in crimson livery stood at watch beside the huge bed. When the young man recognized Alex, he effected a somber expression, his gaze flicking to Freddie's body.

Since they'd been young lads, everyone had always remarked that Freddie and Alex looked almost like twins, but as Alex looked at his brother now, only the same dark golden locks resembled his. Any healthy glow that had shown in Freddie's skin was now pallid and unnatural, like a wax figure. A swift glance at his brother's lifeless face was all Alex could tolerate. He then glared at Freddie's hands.

Someone—had it been Mannings?—had folded his hands over his chest. Alex slowly reached out to touch his brother's fingers. They felt like stones retrieved from the bed of a spring-fed stream. A lone tear trickled down Alex's cheek. He wiped it before turning to Sinjin.

The two nodded and left the chamber.

* * *

Was there a curse on their family? First, his eldest brother had died of a strangulated hernia following a strenuous game of tennis in his second year as reigning duke.

Alex would be the fourth man in four years to hold the title Duke of Fordham. It wasn't supposed to be that way. Not yet thirty years of age, Alex Haversham, the lowly third son, had suddenly been catapulted to the lofty title held by his esteemed father for nearly five decades and by his dead brothers less than two years each.

His hand gripping a glass of brandy, Alex faced his old friend Sinjin across the library desk. Alex reeled from the realization that his brother was dead. Freddie was just a year Alex's senior. "How can a man—a healthy man of thirty—die in his sleep? God knows he didn't share the many vices for which I'm noted. I feel so beastly that I'd been out of charity with Freddie."

Sinjin nodded sympathetically. "Don't beat up on yourself because you two didn't see eye to eye. We're all gentlemen enough to preserve gentility even when we disagree about matters political. Your brother knew you loved him."

"I hope to God he did." Alex's mind wandered back to these past several months and the estrangement that festered between the brothers after Freddie refused to support Alex's Parliamentary campaign. How he wished he could turn back the clock and let his brother know that it mattered not whether they were on opposite benches. A brother was a brother. He swallowed over the lump in his throat.

Now he had no brothers.

Though he'd never been as close to his brothers as he was to Sinjin and Harry Wycliff—the two fellows with whom he'd shared everything during their ten years together at Eton—the three Haversham brothers had always been united by affection for one another, for their parents, and for their adored sisters. All gone now, except for the girls. His stomach twisted at the very idea of breaking such heart-wrenching news to their sisters.

And what about Freddie's betrothed? Alex drew a deep breath. "I shall have to break the distressing intelligence to Lady Georgiana."

"I wouldn't want to be the one to have to tell the lady," Sinjin said.

Alex was well aware that marrying a duke was every lady's ambition. He cringed at the notion of being besieged by mothers trying to foist their insipid daughters on him. Matrimony—his specifically—had never held allure.

He'd always thought the reason Freddie had become betrothed to Lady Georgiana was because a duke was expected to ensure the succession.

He wondered if Lady Georgiana had been in love with Freddie or in love with the idea of being a duchess. Regardless, he dreaded telling the lady about the death of her betrothed.

* * *

That afternoon the solicitor arrived and was shown to the library where Alex was attempting to inure himself to the pain of Freddie's loss with bountiful portions of his brother's best Madeira.

"Ah, Waterman. Good of you to come," Alex said. "Do help yourself." His hand waved to the table of glasses and decanters. While the solicitor was pouring his wine, Alex looked at Sinjin. "Lord Slade, I should like to present Mr. Waterman to you. He's long been solicitor to the Dukes of Fordham."

Mr. Waterman set down the leather case he was carrying, the men shared greetings, and then Alex asked the solicitor to be seated.

"Your grace," Waterman said, "I'm so sorry for your unimaginable loss. I shall endeavor to do everything in my power to help you ascend to your new position."

"I know that all the properties will come to me, but I particularly wanted to learn of any bequests my brother has made so that I can honor them.

Since my brother and I were not terribly close, I was not privy to his plans. In fact, I haven't even met the woman to whom he's betrothed."

"I have taken the liberty of bringing your brother's will." Waterman reached into his leather case and took out a sheet of vellum. "As you know, even though he was a young man, I encouraged him to make his will as soon as he ascended—as I will encourage you to do."

Alex's gut plummeted. *I am the last duke.* Their family must be cursed. Would he be dead like his brothers before he was thirty? He nodded stiffly.

Waterman handed him the will. "You will see your brother had but three bequests. He left two hundred to his valet, two hundred a year to a Mrs. Langston, and he requested that Lady Georgiana Fenton be in charge of his personal papers."

Alex found himself wondering if those personal letters might include correspondence between Freddie and his mistress, the stage actress Mrs. Langston. How peculiar that Freddie's betrothed might read letters from his mistress.

The solicitor frowned, then lowered his voice to reverent tones. "We were to meet this week and draw up the marriage contracts."

Another stab of pain.

Alex eyed Sinjin. "We go to Lady Georgiana in the morning."

This would be worse than writing to the bereaved parents of his soldiers. This would be face to face.

* * *

"I declare, Georgiana, if you keep going out of doors without your bonnet, the duke will take you for a gypsy, and you'll be jilted."

The young lady being admonished eyed her

mother as the dowager sat beside her escritoire, gripping the hilt of the cane that she now depended upon as a babe its mother's milk. Even though she was fifty years of age, Lady Hartworth was still a beautiful woman. She'd been the most highly sought beauty of the *ton* the year she came out. The delicate perfection of her face was matched by the delicacy of her body. A miniature Venus she had been called. Time had changed her little since Gainsborough had painted her thirty years earlier with mounds of powdered hair, hair that now looked much the same, courtesy of gentle aging.

"If Fordham were that abominably shallow," her daughter said, "then I simply would not have him for a husband."

"But, dearest, he's a duke. One can overlook a myriad of faults in a duke."

"But, unlike you, who was *not* born to an aristocratic family, I do not stand in awe of titled personages. I believe, my dearest mother, you were even in awe of Papa, just because he was the Marquess of Hartworth."

"I was, and it's glad I am that you're marrying a king."

Georgiana's eyes widened, and then she started giggling. It wasn't kind to laugh at Mama after her recent affliction, but Georgiana was powerless to stop. "Did you mean to say duke?"

Lady Hartworth slapped her forehead. "Did I say *king?*"

Georgiana nodded.

"I did mean to say duke." Lady Hartworth sighed. "It's always right in my mind, but it just doesn't come out right."

"It will, in time." Mama had nearly made a full

recovery. Georgiana thought back to those frightening days when everyone—including Mama—had been expecting her mother to die—a prospect Georgiana fought with every breath she drew.

"Though a beauty such as you *should* have been able to marry a *king*—not that you would have been the right age for our Regent when he married back in the nineties," Lady Hartworth said. "Still, I don't understand why the Royals can't pluck their brides from the ranks of England's most noble families. Your father, God rest his noble soul, owned more land and had more . . . subjects, or servants, than most of those confounded German principalities and duchies that populate Europe's royal houses."

"Pray, Mama, do not say such things! I assure you I have no desire to be queen of anywhere." Georgiana's eyes narrowed. "What are those brown splotches on your gown?"

"Lady Hartworth groaned. "Chocolate. The *Hellions*. I permitted them to visit my chambers as I read the morning post and sipped my chocolate."

The hellions were Georgiana's brother's young son and daughter. "You cannot expect children under the age five not to make messes."

"But one can expect obedience. I expressly forbade them to jump upon my bed—or any bed—but they ignored me. Their dim-witted mother permits them to do so."

Which was one of the reasons why Georgiana had consented to marry and remove herself from her sister-in-law's sphere. Dim witted aptly described Hester. How smoothly Alsop ran when Mama was mistress here, and now it bore a remarkable resemblance to a lunatic asylum.

Which was a strong impetus to marrying and being mistress of her own home.

In the six years since her debut, Georgiana had spurned every man who attempted to court her. Entirely too particular, she had come to the conclusion she was incapable of a grand passion but had been assured love *would* come once marriage united her to a life's companion.

Since it was well past time for her to marry, Freddie was the most worthy candidate. He was most earnestly attached to her, and he was one of the few men in the kingdom Mama would deem worthy of her only daughter.

Georgiana—without a bonnet—kissed her mother's cheek, snatched her riding crop, and headed toward the front door. Her groom should be waiting there with her mount.

To her great surprise, when she whisked through the open door at the home's entrance, she faced her betrothed, who was giving her bay a great deal of attention. He was accompanied by a man she had never before seen.

"Freddie!" she greeted, a smile on face. Then as she looked into his somber face, she realized this man was not her intended. This must be his radical younger brother, Lord Alex. She'd been told they looked remarkably alike.

Her brows lowered. "You're not Freddie. You must be . . ." Her pulse sped up. From his grim expression, it was obvious he had come bearing grave news. "Something's happened to Freddie."

"Is there somewhere we can talk?" he asked.

By now she was shaking. With a single nod, she led them into the entry corridor of well-worn wooden planks to the library where a fire smoldered in the hearth.

"Please, my lady," said the man she presumed to be Lord Alex, "allow me to pour you a glass of brandy." He strode to the tall table, claimed its only decanter, and started to pour the dark liquid into a glass.

Her heart pounding, all she could manage was a nod. When he handed her the cool glass. she took a long sip, then eyed his melancholy face and spoke with great solemnity. "He's dead."

The new duke nodded. "Permit me to introduce myself. I am his brother Alex."

It was a moment before she could gather her composure. "Was he shot?"

"No. I don't understand it, given his heretofore excellent health, but he died in his sleep."

She could not believe it. She'd seen him just days before his shooting party. Full of life, he seemed much younger than his thirty years. "I refuse to believe him dead. I must see him."

Alex Haversham, the reigning Duke of Fordham, lowered his brows. "I assure you, he's quite dead."

She clapped her hands over her ears. "I refuse to listen to you, your grace. I must see your brother." Her mother would have apoplexy all over again if she heard her stubborn daughter addressing a duke in such a manner.

"I return to Gosingham now. Should you like to accompany me?"

"Indeed I would."

$\mathcal{C}$hapter 2

Alex had been in the Peninsula when Lady Georgiana was presented the same year as his long-married eldest sister Kathryn, now Lady Roxbury. Though he'd not met Lady Georgiana before, Kathryn had written him about the lady's great success. Lady Georgiana Fenton had been considered a beauty and possessed the added bonus of a hefty dowry of twenty thousand, both of which contributed to her considerable popularity with young gentlemen of the *ton*.

He supposed she was good enough looking, but not at all what he had expected. Since Alex had always favored fair complexioned ladies with blond tresses and ample bosom, he was almost taken aback to see that his brother's intended was possessed of mahogany-coloured hair, eyes almost black, and a skin more like what one would see in a Spaniard than in the daughter of an English marquess.

Alex and his brother *had* always held vastly different tastes. As a duke, Freddie could have won the hand of any beauty in the kingdom. Why in the devil had Freddie chosen this sharp-tongued woman who was past the first blush of youth? What had Freddie been thinking? The lady was in want of those qualities every man desired in a wife: obedience, agreeableness—and womanly curvature.

Lady Georgiana *had* been more than a year younger when she and Freddie had announced their betrothal. Just before they were to have married, her mother had been stricken with apoplexy and nearly died. It was to Lady Georgiana's credit that she refused to leave her mother's side then or during the months of the dowager's slow recovery which followed. Freddie had conceded that the marriage would be indefinitely postponed, either for Lady Hartworth's convalescence or for a mourning period if the mother had died.

Before Lady Georgiana left Alsop Hall with him and Sinjin, she had informed him that her mother had insisted she be accompanied by her lady's maid. Therefore, the mute-acting French woman who looked a decade younger than her mistress rode in the carriage with them for the three-hour journey back to Gosingham.

He felt compelled to attempt conversation with Lady Georgiana. Glad he was that she had not turned into a watering pot, yet he questioned the lady's attachment to his brother. Had she not been in love with Freddie? Or was she the rare female who could manage to keep a tight control over her emotions? She had not shed a single tear.

"I pray that your mother has made a satisfactory recovery?" he said to her once the coach had reached the main posting road a few miles from Alsop.

"We've been vastly pleased with her progress. Her speech is almost back to where it was, and she is now able to walk with the use of a cane. Thank you, your grace, for asking."

"How long has it been?" Alex asked. "Since she

fell ill?"

"It was a year in November."

More than a year. Freddie was a patient soul.

"Your mother suffered from sudden apoplexy?" Sinjin asked.

The lady nodded.

"I daresay if she's made so successful a recovery," Sinjin said, "she has received excellent care. When my grandfather was stricken, we attributed his reversal to my grandmother's excellent ministrations on his behalf. She was devoted to him in every way. She not only never left his bedside, but she also forced him to try to speak, to try to walk. She never considered that he wouldn't experience a full recovery."

"Who was the person responsible for your mother's progress?" Alex asked Lady Georgiana.

Alex noticed that the maid eyed her mistress. It was a moment before the mistress responded with a shrug. "I daresay my overbearingly didactic self rather forced poor Mama not to succumb to her infirmity."

"You should not malign yourself," Alex said. "Your determination is most commendable."

Lady Georgiana eyed Sinjin. "Lord Slade, how old was your grandfather when he was struck down?"

Sinjin pursed his lips, his brows dipping. "Let me see . . . yes, I remember. He was still in his fifties—a month shy of his sixtieth birthday."

"Mama was but eight and forty," she said. "Far too young, I thought, to become a dependent invalid. Tell me, Lord Slade, did your grandfather fully regain his speech?"

"Yes, he did."

"Mama's speech is now only slightly impaired,

but she's developed the silliest practice of knowing exactly what she's going to say, but the wrong words come out. For example, she'll look right at the toad in the hole and say she wants that pig's foot. I try not to laugh, but sometimes her statements are epically humorous."

"You should not feel badly. The fact both of you know what she meant to say attests to her mental acuity," Alex said.

She nodded, a faint smile rendering her face something quite lovely. He didn't know if he'd ever seen teeth so extraordinarily white. Her attention then returned to Sinjin. "What about your grandfather's ability to walk?"

"His left side remained weak, but he never let it slow him. He refuses to use a cane."

"I believe Mama could walk without her cane, but she's afraid of falling. I tell her she needs to test herself or she'll become dependent on the cane."

"Then you're a stern taskmaster," Alex commented. Given this woman's unemotional reaction to the death of her betrothed, Alex was not surprised to learn that Lady Georgiana could appear callous.

She glared at him. "Nothing is gained from coddling."

This woman reminded Alex of Kathryn, the eldest of his four sisters. They were both pragmatic. It took no great effort to imagine this woman ordering about a parcel of younger siblings (as Kathryn had done) in the same way one would position tin soldiers. Unlike Lady Georgiana, though, Kathryn easily shed tears over those she loved. After Alex's eldest brother had died when Alex was serving in the Peninsula, he'd been told

Kathryn had been almost inconsolable upon Richard's death. And in the letter she'd sent him last week, she revealed how relieved she'd been when her youngest daughter's fever broke. "I stood bawling over her bed," she wrote.

He could not imagine this stoic woman sitting across the carriage from him ever bawling. He eyed her. "Now's as good a time as any to tell you that you were the subject of a bequest in my brother's will."

"Freddie knew I did not need money."

"It wasn't money he left you."

Her brows rose.

"It was his papers," Alex said.

"His papers? Like his personal correspondence?"

"Yes."

"I shall be honored to undertake that task."

"I suppose some of them will go in the Fordham archives in the Gosingham basement."

She nodded. "Though reading his letters will make me melancholy, it is the very type of activity which suits my temperament."

Alex could well believe the woman thrived on being in charge of things. Something in her demeanor indicated that she was likely well organized. She did not appear to be the type of woman who filled her head with fashion. Even though her family was one of the wealthiest in the kingdom, the dress she wore was faded, and its print was of the style popular a few seasons earlier. At least that's what his sisters had imparted to him.

Perhaps he should steer the conversation to a brighter topic. "It appeared that as we arrived as Alsop, you were about to go riding. You obviously have a good eye for horse flesh. A very fine bay you had."

"His grace is horse mad," Sinjin said. "He can see the most minute difference in two horses that look identical to the rest of us."

She forced a smile. "As fond as Freddie was of horses, he said you were stupendously knowledgeable about the beasts, and given the Fordhams' legendary stables, that is towering praise."

He did not know how to respond without sounding conceited, so he said nothing.

After a lengthy lull in conversion, Sinjin redirected the topic. "I hate to remind you of your grievous loss, old fellow, but has it occurred to you that you'll now have to give up your hard-earned seat in the House of Commons since you'll be joining me in the House of Lords?"

"I hadn't given it a thought." Alex drew his breath. "There will have to be a by-election to fill my seat."

"As Duke of Fordham," Sinjin said, "you'll be in a position to sponsor your own candidates."

Alex nodded. "Edward Coke's the very man to take my place."

"He'll be perfect. I was sorry he lost last year."

"As was I. He's a fine chap."

"And he'll vote exactly as Wycliff tells him to vote."

Alex felt Lady Georgiana's scathing glare. "Forgive me if it seems I'm profiting in any way from my brother's death," he said, eying her. "I would give every farthing I could ever own to bring him back."

"It's understandable that you'll profit from his death," she said. "What is unforgivable is that you will vote against everything your brother believed in."

Neither he nor Sinjin had a retort. It was true that he and Freddie were on opposite ends of the political spectrum. He loved his brother—but not enough to turn his back on his own ideology.

The only sound to be heard for the remainder of the journey was the monotonous churning of the coach wheels and the occasional cracking of the coachman's whip.

It was during the last remnants of dusk that the coach rattled up the tree-lined path to Lincolnshire's grandest country house. Gosingham Hall had been built by the first duke more than two hundred years previously. In the last century, Capability Brown had selected these beech trees that now struggled to bloom after an exceedingly harsh winter. By next month the drive would be shaded by their canopy.

When Alex beheld the magnificent house sprawling atop the hill's crest and crowned by a gold dome, tears sprang to his eyes. *This is all mine now.* He had never thought to be master of such a place, and the very notion terrified him. Had he any expectations of inheriting, he would have made a greater effort to learn more about the generations of Havershams who'd come before him and to learn about their various contributions to the family and to this colossal monument of stone and glass.

The tears he suppressed represented so much more than his overwhelming inadequacies. He mourned his parents. Most of all, he mourned his brothers who were cut down in the prime of life.

In the distance he could see the prodigious stables where the brothers had spent so much time. They had fashioned their own steeplechase course, and even though Alex was the youngest, he'd always won. What good times they'd had during those lazy days of summer. His eyes moistened.

The carriage drew up in front of Gosingham's portico, and the coachman let down the steps and opened the carriage door. It was then that Alex remembered the coachman's son had been accidentally killed the previous year at one of Freddie's shooting parties. They never did learn whose bullet had struck down the ten-year-old lad. "Thank you, John," Alex said, pausing to eye the man with heart-felt sincerity. "I've never been able to say how sorry I was about your boy's death."

The coachman's head inclined. Grief was still etched on his craggy face. The loss of the son who'd come so late in life and who had for so many years brought a smile to the old man's face and lightened his step, nearly put the old man in his grave. Alex clasped a hand to his shoulder. For that second, the two men were joined by their respective grief.

* * *

She hadn't seen Gosingham Hall until they crested the hill. Its gold dome shimmered beneath the diffused moonlight. There was no lovelier house in all of Lincolnshire. This was to have become her home. She felt as if a gold sovereign lodged in her throat.

That disappointment was pushed from her thoughts by the greater, all-encompassing bereavement that obliterated all other thoughts from her mind. Freddie, dear thoughtful Freddie, was dead. It was as if a huge void hollowed her, robbing her of every cell, every feeling. All that was left was a vast numbness.

How she regretted that she'd not been able to see the dear man happily wed before his life was so cruelly cut short. He had craved domesticity as heartily as other men pursued debauchery. She felt guilty she had delayed their marriage. Why had she persisted in keeping Mama at Alsop and avoiding marriage? It wasn't as if she couldn't have brought her mother to Gosingham once she married the duke. She could have overseen Mama's care once she became Freddie's duchess. Why had she so stubbornly clung to her spinsterhood?

She'd been startled at how closely the new duke resembled Freddie. Even though he appeared pleasant enough, she could not admire the man. He had caused Freddie a great deal of distress. He was a Whig, and Freddie had been a Tory. All her family were Tories.

Inside Gosingham, they were greeted by a butler carrying a brace of candles to complement the wall sconces, which were all lighted. "I wasn't sure your grace would return tonight. Forgive me for taking the liberty of allowing the other servants to retire for the night. If your grace is hungry, I can awaken the cook."

"That won't be necessary," Alex said. "Lady Georgiana's cook packed us something to eat in the coach."

"Very good, your grace."

"It's been an exhausting day. Lord Slade and I will go directly to our chambers. All that we require is that you show Lady Georgiana and her maid to their rooms."

"I shall put Lady Georgiana in the yellow

room," Mannings said with a nod.

She followed the aged servant up the broad marble staircase to the second floor where her host and Lord Slade bid her goodnight. Mannings continued down a corridor carpeted with a Turkish rug and stopped midway to open the door to the yellow chamber. "Had I known you were coming, my lady, I would have requested a fire be laid." He walked into the dark room and began to light every candle.

Though it was still quite dark, she could see that silken draperies of pale yellow hung from three tall casements as well as on the high tester bed. The silk coverlet upon the huge bed combined the same pale yellow with a pattern of soft green acanthus leaves. It was an inviting room, and like the new duke, all she required was to climb into the comforting bed.

"I am quite certain I shall be fast asleep before a fire could possibly warm this chamber," she told the butler. "The only thing I request is that you show my maid her quarters, then send her back to me."

Less than five minutes later, Angelique returned and helped Georgiana out of her traveling clothes. After Angelique brushed out her hair, Georgiana climbed atop the bed, and Angelique drew the draperies around her mistress's bed before she left.

As tired as Georgiana was, sleep eluded her. In the morning she would view the lifeless body of the man with whom she had planned to spend the rest of her life.

Though she had always been a realist, some child-like side of her had emerged today, telling her that these people were wrong. Freddie was not dead. They all had to be mistaken. He was young. He was full of life. He was in excellent health. He had none of the vices of his philandering younger brother. He could not be dead.

Is that why she was going to put herself through such a tortuous ordeal? Her stomach roiled. Her breath grew short. She dreaded what would occur in the morning.

Yet it couldn't be worse than this day had been—and still was.

* * *

She hadn't been able to sleep, so when the duke rapped at her door just past dawn, she was already fully dressed. She opened the door herself and observed him. He, too, was dressed, and judging by the puffiness beneath his eyes, she knew he'd also been unable to sleep.

"Should you like to see my brother now?" he asked. "We men will bury him today."

Burying Freddie. Those words, spoken so matter-of-factly, wiped away her childish denial. This was not some shattering dream. This was real. Freddie was dead.

She nodded solemnly.

As the two of them climbed the stairs, he said, "This won't be as unpleasant as it was when I first viewed him. The chamber was then in darkness. I've instructed the servants to draw the draperies and open the windows. Freddie disliked the dark."

Windows open or not, approaching the bed where lifeless Freddie lay was the most difficult thing she'd ever done. No amount of hopeful thoughts could reverse the finality of his untimely death.

In spite of her queasy stomach, she forced herself to study the face that had once looked so much like that of the brother who stood beside her but now looked so horribly alien. His deep golden hair had been combed into the same fashionable style he always wore. His eyes were closed. His skin had lost the color of a living being. She willed herself not to be sick, not to cry.

She drew a deep breath and moved closer, reaching out to open one of his eyes. A wrenching feeling lurched when she realized how stiff his skin was, but she managed to open the eye closest to her.

She had allowed herself to imagine that once he could see her, he would spring to life. How well she remembered his lichen-colored eyes. The color had not changed, but now his eye—except for the iris—was almost a solid crimson.

She quickly closed it.

Her gaze moved to the pillow upon which his head rested. Small puddles of dried blood had pooled there.

"Someone smothered this man to death," she said with conviction.

$\mathcal{C}$hapter 3

Alex drew the delusional woman aside and led her to the adjoining study. "What the devil are you saying?"

"I know as sure as I know I'm standing here in Gosingham Hall that Freddie was smothered as he slept."

Her words cut through him as surely as a rapier. "How could you possibly know such a thing?"

"While working with my mother's rehabilitation, I became particularly interested in studies of anatomy. I've read the works of the surgeon Douglas MacKay. He cites a death by suffocation. Two signs can confirm such a death." She paused.

His heart pounded. His hands slickened. "Yes?"

"Bloodied eyeballs and blood upon the pillow from drainage during the horrible, premeditated deed." Her voice weakened, and then she drew a deep breath and faced him with renewed vigor. "Who wanted your brother dead?"

"No one! You must know as well as I that my brother had no enemies."

She glared at him.

Good Lord! Did this unbalanced woman think he had murdered his own brother? "I beg that you mention this no more—especially around the

servants. I'll speak to you on the matter later—
after we've given my brother a proper burial."

"I must insist that a surgeon sees him before
he's buried."

* * *

Their neighbor, Lord Harold Barnstaple, was
the first to call and offer condolences over
Freddie's death. As Alex strode down the broad
marble hall, it occurred to him that death did not
abide by time restrictions. Normally, this would be
far too early to pay a morning call, but mourners
sought other mourners without regard to the
hour. Had Barnstaple just heard?

The viscount awaited Alex in the library,
standing there with his hat in his hand. Alex did
not precisely know his age, but he was a year or
two older than Richard and had been Alex's eldest
brother's childhood playmate. So he must be
approaching five and thirty. He looked older,
perhaps because his love of riding and shooting
had leathered his skin. His hairline, too, was
receding.

When their eyes met, a somber expression
stole over Barnstaple's face, and he slowly shook
his head. "I am bereft of words to describe my
great sadness over your brother's passing."

Alex's head dipped. "Good of you to come. Do
let me have the footman collect your hat."

"No, I'm not staying. I have no wish to intrude.
I suppose I was in hopes you would tell me this
was some evil jest. I can't believe Fordham's gone.
He was in such jolly spirits during the shooting
party. He seemed perfectly fit. Pray, what can
have happened?"

"I wish we knew. When his man entered his
chamber yesterday morning he found my brother

dead in his bed of apparent natural causes."

"Good Lord, I must have just left!"

Alex nodded. "So I have been told. All of you were traveling home by the time his death was discovered."

Barnstaple kept staring at him as if in disbelief. "What woes have befallen your family in the past few years."

"Indeed."

"I . . . suppose he'll be buried beside Richard?"

Barnstaple, because of his lifelong friendship with Richard, was the only person outside of their family who persisted in calling Alex's eldest brother by his Christian name after he became the Duke of Fordham. Even speaking of him now caused Barnstaple's voice to tremble with emotion.

"Yes, this afternoon."

"I shall be there." The affected neighbor turned on his heel and left.

* * *

Georgiana could not eat breakfast. She had not been able to swallow a single bite since she had learned of Freddie's death. She had joined his grace—it was painful to think of another with Freddie's title—and his friend at breakfast, but Fordham was called away when a neighbor called to pay his respects.

Fifteen minutes later he returned. "Lord Barnstaple had just heard about Freddie," he explained. "He'd been here the night Freddie died, but the members of the shooting party all left the following morning—not knowing that Freddie was dead."

The surgeon arrived after breakfast. Alex knew that no matter what Todd had been doing, a summons from the Duke of Fordham always took precedence.

Once more Alex would have to behold his poor, dead brother. He'd thought viewing Freddie's body would have been easier in a sun-filled room. But light did nothing to alter the fact his brother was cold and dead.

"As you have probably heard," Alex began, "my brother died in his sleep the night before last. Since there was nothing you could have done to revive him, we felt no need to consult you."

They had climbed the stairs to the second level.

"But now?" Todd asked, winded.

The white-haired Todd had been serving the Fordham family since the days of Alex's grandfather. The surgeon had probably witnessed every type of death possible in these past five decades.

Alex's voice shook when he spoke. "My brother's fiancée believes he was suffocated."

Todd nodded. "Suffocation is almost impossible to detect. In some cases blood will appear on the pillow used to do the deed—but that can be easily hidden by removing the pillow of its covering."

"There's blood on my brother's pillow." That someone deliberately smothered the life from Freddie sent Alex's gut plummeting. It was bad enough that he was dead, but murdered? Fury bolted through him.

Todd stopped and turned to Alex, a grave expression on his face. "Does the blood appear to have come from the orifices?"

Alex shrugged. He was embarrassed to admit he hadn't examined the pillow. "I couldn't look."

The surgeon clasped Alex's shoulder. "It's my job to look; you need not."

"Then I shan't."

When Todd approached Freddie's bed, Alex stayed several feet behind, watching the surgeon. Just as Lady Georgiana had done, Todd lifted Freddie's eyelid and studied what it revealed. Alex thought he was also opening Freddie's mouth, but he could only see Todd's back. Which was all Alex cared to see.

Lastly, the surgeon lifted Freddie's head, removed the pillow, and examined it.

Then he came to Alex. "If I were a wagering man, I'd bet that your brother was murdered in his sleep."

Freddie felt as if a cannon ball had hurled into him. It was a moment before he could speak. "If it's the last thing I ever do, I will find out who did this."

Todd nodded solemnly. "I shall keep these findings private."

"Tell no one."

* * *

Georgiana watched from her chamber window. Every male at Gosingham Hall from the lowliest groom to the new duke walked in the funeral procession from the magnificent manor house to the family's temple-like mausoleum three quarters of a mile away. The village priest, dressed in a black cassock, led. He was followed by the new duke and his friend, Lord Slade. Even at such a distance, she could hear the bells from the village church tolling for the shire's loftiest aristocrat.

As the bells rang, male villagers, some dressed in simple homespun, joined in order to show their respect for the man whose family had owned every plot of land, every crofter's hut, every shop in the village for the past two centuries.

Before the new duke returned, she pulled herself together. She'd been asking herself who had the strongest motive for wanting Freddie dead. Who had the most to gain?

The answer was simple. Alex Haversham, the ninth Duke of Fordham.

* * *

He felt lower than an adder's belly after laying his brother to rest in the family vault. For eternity Freddie's remains would lie next to Richard's.

Alex would be next. Would he make it past his thirtieth year? Was Freddie's murderer lying in wait to kill Alex?

"Here," Sinjin said. "You need brandy." The two men took their drinks and sat before the fire in Gosingham's library. The day had grown colder. By the time they had left the mausoleum, the skies had blackened. It was as if earth mourned his brother's loss.

"You need to come back to London," Sinjin said. "Being in this house of melancholy will keep your spirits low."

"You don't know how low." Alex turned and eyed his dark-haired friend. Sinjin's eyes were so dark, they looked black. Just like Lady Georgiana's. Infuriating woman. "I cannot leave."

"Give me one good reason why you must stay."

How difficult it was to say. It was a moment before he could respond. "Freddie was murdered. Smothered by a pillow as he slept."

Sinjin's eyes widened. "How could you possibly know such a thing?"

Alex explained Lady Georgiana's suspicions and the surgeon's confirmation. "And the pity of it is," he concluded, "I think she believes I'm the killer!"

"I'll talk to her."

"The lady was already predisposed to despise me."

"That would mean that Freddie must have maligned you when speaking to her."

Alex shrugged. "Possibly. But there is the fact the Marquesses of Hartworth are staunch Tories."

"There is that." Sinjin took a swig of his brandy.

"I care not what that wretched woman thinks of me, but I'm determined to do everything I can to find out who murdered my brother."

"It must have been one of the fellows at the shooting party."

"Then we must make a list of those attending." It still seemed inconceivable that anyone would wish his brother dead.

There was a knock upon the library door, and before he could respond, Lady Georgiana entered the chamber. "May I come in?"

Alex stood as he always did when greeting a lady. "Please do. I've been wanting to tell you what the surgeon said. May I offer you Madeira?"

"No thank you," she answered stiffly as she came to sit on the settee next to Sinjin.

Alex knew she'd rather sit in a bed of vipers than next to him. He took a long drink of the brandy. "It appears, my lady, you were correct in your assumptions about my brother's death."

For the first instant since he'd met her, she lost her composure. "Would that I were wrong," she murmured. Then she dissolved into tears.

To his knowledge, this woman had not shed a tear over Freddie's unexpected death. Until now. And now it was as if the floodgates had collapsed. Her shoulders heaved. Great mournful sobs had been unleashed and showed no signs of retreating.

He had loathed her a moment earlier. Now he wanted to soothe her grief. Strangely, he understood why she had suddenly been overcome with her grief. For he felt the same. He moved to her, offered his large chambray handkerchief, and stood by solemnly as she attempted to blot her tears. He set a gentle hand on her shoulder. He was unprepared for her delicacy. She no longer seemed the overbearing wench.

"I . . . I don't know what's gotten into me." Sniff. Sniff. "I'm never such a ninny."

"You're not a ninny," he said tenderly. "Your reactions are completely normal under so sorrowful an occurrence."

Sniff. Sniff.

"I vow to you I will never stop until my brother's murderer is brought to justice."

"Just before you came in," Sinjin said to her, "Fordham was saying he needed to make a list of all those attending his brother's shooting party. One of them has to be responsible for the reprehensible act."

It seemed queer to hear Sinjin so easily slip into calling Alex by his new title, especially since, after all these years, he and Wycliff still referred to Sinjin by the his school-boy name.

She gave one last sniff and blew her nose. "I can help with the list. Freddie wrote me, telling me all those he was expecting. I brought it with me since it's the last communication I ever received from him." Her voice cracked as she spoke.

Perhaps she wasn't as cold as he'd formerly thought. Though he believed he knew perfectly well who had attended the shooting party he wanted her to feel part of the inquiry. "Shall I have Mannings ask your maid to bring it to you?"

She nodded solemnly. "Have him tell Angelique it's in my reticule. It's the only letter there."

Alex rang for the servant, then went to the desk and took out a sheet of vellum. "Our neighbor, Lord Barnstable, was a member of the shooting party. He learned of Freddie's death sometime after he'd returned to Mayfield Manor. I shall put him at the top of the list, though I'm certain he cannot be a suspect. Known him all my life. He's not that much older than Freddie, and they've always been friends."

Mannings returned and gave a sheet of foolscap to the lady. Alex watched her as she unfolded it. Though her eyes misted, she kept a firm grasp onto her composure. "Yes, I see Lord Barnstaple on here. Counting the late duke, there were just six men in attendance—besides yourself and Lord Slade."

"Who were *not* included in the shooting party."

The late duke. It did sound less personal than Freddie, less painful for its lack of familiarity. "Freddie's friend Lord Pomfoy came."

Her dark eyes lowered. "Yes, he's listed here."

Alex added Lord Pomfoy's name to his own list. "And there was our cousin, Robert Cecil. He's mad for shooting."

She nodded. "Yes, he was of the party."

Alex sighed as he wrote down his cousin's name. "I shall have to notify him of Freddie's death. And our sisters, too. I shan't look forward to that."

Her brows lowered in sympathy.

"I wish I could help you, old fellow," Sinjin said, "but I know you'll want to do that yourself."

"I believe I will go back to London with you," Alex said. "I must tell the girls."

"Yes," Sinjin said, "I need to return. Parliament calls."

"Not to mention your bride." It had only been a matter of weeks since Sinjin had married Jane Featherstone, making both of Alex's best friends blissfully happy in marriage.

"The only one on the list I know, other than Lord Pomfoy, is Lord Hickington," she said.

"Can't say that I know the fellow." Alex glanced at Sinjin. The two having just arrived at Gosingham the previous day, they hadn't mingled in the shooting party.

"I used to see him at White's," Sinjin said.

Alex wrote down the name Hickington, then eyed her. "You know him through Freddie?"

She shook her head. "No." After a noticeable pause, she added, "I've known him for some years."

Alex wondered if he'd been a suitor of hers. Her evasive response left much room for interpretation. "Let's see who's last on the list."

"Sir Arthur Fontaine," she said.

"Ah, yes." Alex wrote on the vellum. "The friend who took Mrs. Lang . . ." He clamped shut his mouth. He couldn't bring up Freddie's former mistress in the presence of his fiancée.

"You needn't guard your tongue in my presence," she said. "I know of Freddie's lady bird."

Sinjin's brows lowered. "He spoke to you of such matters?"

"No, of course not. But a lady learns about such things."

"Then such knowledge will no doubt make it easier on you as you go through my brother's correspondence. And you must know he ended the association upon his betrothal to you."

Her eyes misting, she nodded solemnly.

He wrote down the name Sir Arthur Fontaine, who had become the new protector of the actress Mrs. Langston after Freddie dismissed her.

"Now then, let's discuss possible motives," Ales said. "In the case of murder, the two chief motivators are for gain of possessions or for love. I realize I'm the one who would benefit the most from my brother's death, but I am also the person most devastated by his loss—yourself excluded. I have never in my life wanted to be a duke. I will own, having a fortune's attractive, but having the responsibilities and stewardship of a dukedom were burdens I never would have sought."

"Not to mention that you loved your brother, and you're one of the kindest men I've ever known—and I've know you since you were seven years of age." Sinjin scowled at Lady Georgiana. "I assure you, his grace is incapable of murder."

"I prefer to make up my own mind," she said, glaring at Alex. "I have a question to ask you."

Alex quirked a brow.

"You weren't of the shooting party. Do you not think it suspicious that you showed up on the very day Freddie was murdered?"

"Now see here!" Sinjin roared. "How dare you impugn so fine a man with your unfounded accusations."

"I'm not making accusations. I'm merely trying to determine the truth." She glared at Alex. "Why did you come to Gosingham?"

"I'll answer that," Sinjin said. "The two of us have been charged with drafting a bill supporting penal reform, and since our lives in London are so busy and finding a quiet spot nearly impossible, I am the one who suggested we come to Gosingham. Freddie, as you must know, normally lives a quiet, reclusive life. Or lived."

"As I said, I'm not making accusations. I'm only trying to discover the truth."

Alex wanted to redirect the conversation. Any tenderness he'd held for Lady Georgiana moments ago had now leeched away by her abrasive manner. "I wonder if Freddie possessed something someone else wanted."

"There's his valet," Sinjin offered. "Does he not stand to gain two hundred from your brother's death?"

"Yes, but Freddie was paying him a handsome hundred a year already, and I believe the man was most satisfied with his position. Few jobs are as prestigious as serving as valet to a duke."

"There is that," Sinjin conceded.

"Did the late duke leave a legacy for Mrs. Langston?" Lady Georgiana asked.

Alex did not want to answer. One simply did not discuss a mistress with a man's intended. For that matter, one never discussed mistresses with well-born ladies. Soon, though, Lady Georgiana was bound to find out—from Freddie's own papers—the extent of his brother's involvement with the well-known actress. Finally, Alex nodded. "Mrs. Langston will get two hundred a year."

Sinjin's gaze swept from Lady Georgiana to

Alex. "Do you suppose the woman came to the shooting party?"

"I'll ask Mannings," Alex said.

"Is not Sir Arthur her new protector?" Sinjin asked. "I doubt the fellow would approve of her renewing an acquaintance with her former paramour."

"I suspect the new duke has more knowledge of such matters," she snapped.

"The lady imbues me with qualities I do not possess. As the penniless third son, I've never had the funds to be responsible for another's upkeep."

Sinjin chuckled. "A man as popular with the ladies as you . . ." He stopped himself and eyed the chamber's lone female occupant. "Forgive me. I forgot there was a lady in the room."

"We will never make any progress," she said, "if you two defer to my gender. I have a brother who has always treated me as if I'm one of the fellows. I assure you, nothing you can say will bring a blush to my cheeks."

Alex could well believe that. She was unlike any wilting-flower female with whom he'd ever been acquainted. "Can either of you think of any possession Freddie owned that was worth killing for? And especially by any of the five men who were at Gosingham his last night?"

"Seven," she corrected, her voice as chilled as ice.

"I beg that you remove Lord Slade from your suspects," Alex said. "A more noble man has never drawn breath."

"Oh, come now," Sinjin protested.

She glared at the both of them.

The room went silent for a moment. Finally she offered, "Perhaps there's another materialistic motive. Freddie had recently paid a great deal of money for a Raphael. Perhaps we could find out if anyone else had been desirous of obtaining it."

Alex made a note on the paper. "I cannot think of anyone besides me who stands to gain substantially from my brother's death."

"Then let's move on to history's most prominent motive for murder—love," Sinjin said.

"Perhaps Mrs. Langston was devastated that Freddie was leaving her to marry me."

"That sounds plausible." Alex wrote down the actress's name with a question mark beside it. "It's not unheard of for a duke to offer marriage to an actress. Perhaps the woman had aspirations of becoming a duchess."

"There's also the possibility that one of Lady Georgiana's spurned lovers wanted to clear the Duke of Fordham from standing in his path."

She laughed. "I have no spurned lovers."

"Not true, my lady," Sinjin said. "I was witness to your vast success the season you came out. I can attest that men numbering into the dozens wished to claim your hand in marriage. Can you refute that?"

"I cannot, but I stand behind my statement. I have had no lovers."

"But what of persistent suitors?" Alex asked.

She did not respond for a moment. "You have me there. A few men have stubbornly refused to concede that they've been unable to claim my dowry."

"You modestly discount your own charms, my lady," Alex said. "Would any of these stubborn men be on this list, my lady?"

She hesitated. "Lord Hickington, actually, but the man would not kill for a mere twenty thousand."

"My dear lady," Sinjin said, "I beg you not say *mere* twenty thousand."

"Men have killed for much less," Alex said.

"It's not as if I've even seen Lord Hickington since I became betrothed to your brother."

"Still, it's something to consider. What other motives can there be?" Alex asked.

"Revenge. Retaliation," Sinjin offered.

"I know of no one who might have had a grudge against my brother," Alex said, eying her. "Do you?"

She shook her head. Then a moment later, she held up her hand. "There was something he felt terribly guilty over. . ."

"What?" Alex asked.

"The death of his coachman's lad. Freddie feared it may have been his bullet that killed the boy."

Alex's gut plummeted. Freddie had never admitted that to him. Poor Freddie. Poor John. No father had ever been more devoted than John Prine was to his lad. What a terrible loss it had been. With anguish, Alex picked up his pen and wrote down the coachman's name.

"What else are we missing?" Sinjin asked. "What other motive?"

"Jealousy," she said. "Although I've always thought only mentally deranged persons would kill for jealousy."

"I would agree with you," Alex said.

She regarded him with twinkling eyes. "So you are in agreement with me and it didn't emasculate you?"

He chuckled heartily. This woman could read him entirely too thoroughly.

"Back to this jealousy theory," Sinjin said. "There's a fine line between that and love. Spurned lovers and all of that."

"But there are other kinds of jealousy," Alex pointed out. "For example, it would only be normal if Lord Pomfoy, Freddie's best friend, were jealous of my brother. Freddie was heir to a vast estate and could have anything his heart desired. Pomfoy's estate is considerably smaller."

"And your brother was handsome, whilst his friend is not in the least," Sinjin added.

Lady Georgiana smiled. "You could hardly expect Fordham to admit his brother was handsome, given that the two brothers so vastly resembled one another."

He'd been stunned she, too, had slipped into calling him Fordham. It must have been painful for her. He masked his surprise with a playful retort. "I take it, Lady Georgiana, you found my brother handsome."

"I refuse to answer. I shouldn't want to further inflate the ego of the new duke who's infamous for his female conquests."

In spite of her words, he realized the stiffness that had stood between them like an iron wall was melting away. He dismissed her comment about his flirtations. "So, are we saying it's possible Lord Pomfoy could have murdered my brother out of pure jealousy?"

The other two shook their heads. "Not probable. Unless he were a mad man, and I find that unlikely," Sinjin said.

"Not to mention I've known him most of my life, and he's a fine fellow," Alex said.

"Anything else?" Sinjin asked. "Anyone else?"

Alex shook his head. "I can't think of anything.

Tomorrow, we'll return to London and start making discreet inquiries—after I break the wretched news of Freddie's death to my sisters."

"I'm coming to London, too," Lady Georgiana said. "I'll bring Freddie's correspondence to sort through whilst I'm there. Perhaps my presence might help when you speak to your sisters. I'm quite close to them."

Alex had hoped he'd seen enough of Lady Georgiana. "You will leave your mother?"

"No. I'll see to it she also comes to London. She needs a break from her grandchildren. They are ill-behaved monsters."

How could one speak of her own nieces and nephews in such a manner? What a paradox Lady Georgiana Fenton was. Large doses of vinegar with a dollop of honey.

Though he did not fancy spending more time with his brother's affianced, her presence might make it easier to break the sorrowful news to his sisters.

$\mathcal{C}$hapter 4

Lady Georgiana Fenton was singular indeed. No other woman of Alex's acquaintance could rush off to the Capital without spending days overseeing the packing of portmanteaus heaped with gowns, hats, shoes, and gloves for every purpose. Yet this lady had no qualms about setting off in his carriage with only the single valise she'd brought to Gosingham—and two bulging valises of Freddie's correspondence. She still wore that faded muslin dress his sisters wouldn't think suitable to give to a servant. He was vaguely aware of the scent he'd come to associate with her. Roses.

The lady expressed full confidence in her maid's ability to pack her trunks back at Alsop and in her mother's competent maid to see that the marchioness's journey to London in a few days' time was as smooth as French satin.

After the lady, Alex, and Sinjin were settled in the coach for the long trip, she said, "This is the first time I've been away from Mama since her affliction."

Alex was not pleased that he would have to share his carriage with her. A pity she hadn't returned to Alsop to oversee her mother's and her own preparations for London. "Your mother won't mind having to travel all the way to London alone?" he asked.

"She won't be alone. Emma—her maid—is extremely capable. Mama's had her ever since she was a bride."

"And it *has* been over a year since your mother fell ill," Sinjin said. "It's time to give her some independence."

The lady nodded. "I agree. And I think London will be good for her."

"Get her away from the monsters," Alex said with a wink.

"If you just looked at my niece and nephew, you would believe them cherubs, but they have most assuredly earned the description of *hellions* through no fault of their own."

"Whose fault then?" Sinjin asked.

"The present marchioness indulges them exceedingly. They are permitted to do anything they wish. I daresay if they wished to wallow in a pig sty, their witless mother would be most agreeable."

"Then you and your mother will most certainly enjoy getting away," Alex said. "You'll stay at Hartworth House in London?"

"Yes, we sent a courier to London to notify the staff there." She pulled from her bag a book. "If you gentlemen wish to speak about Parliament or other manly things, go right ahead. I shan't be disturbed. I've brought my own diversion."

Sinjin shook his head and stared at her with disbelief. "The motion doesn't make you ill when you read in a carriage?"

"Not at all."

A most singular woman, to be sure.

* * *

When night fell they stopped at an inn for dinner and a clean bed. As inns went, the three-story Howling Dog was large. It was tucked right in the midst of the thriving market town of Stanbury. Alex's servants had provided clean linen for the three of them. A hot dinner was so promptly served in his private parlor, he suspected his servants had thrown around his new ducal title.

Their female companion had hardly spoken during the day's long journey, so engrossed had she been in her book. "Pray, my lady, what book has captured your attention so thoroughly?" Alex asked once they sat down to dinner.

She put down her glass and eyed him across the small oak table. The blazing fire to her back perfectly framed her, her dark tresses giving off reddish glints. He was struck by how disarranged her hair was. Now he understood the value of a lady's maid.

"I was reading the memoirs of the late Lord Chatham," she answered. "I know they're old, but my Papa had enjoyed them as a young man."

"A pity Lord Chatham's son did not live long enough to write his," Alex said. "How old was he when he died?" He eyed Sinjin. "We were at Eton when he died so unexpectedly."

"William Pitt the Younger died at forty-six," Lady Georgiana answered.

"Sinjin, Wycliff, and I actually heard him address Parliament when we were students," Alex said. "He was a superior orator—though, of course, none of us were inclined to agree with him."

She wrinkled her nose in distaste. "Because you're Whigs."

Alex nodded.

"My father was and my brother is a staunch

Tory. Perhaps that's why I was drawn to read about the elder Pitt," she said.

This was the first time since he'd met her that he really looked at her face, and to his astonishment, he realized she was beautiful. He'd originally dismissed her on the basis of her darker colouring and lack of bosom. Now, though, he found her large dark eyes framed with long lashes uncommonly expressive. If her lashes dipped while she was speaking, he found it seductive. He found himself watching her mouth, admiring her perfect teeth. Did they appear whiter than others' because her complexion was darker? His gaze feathered over the features of her flawless face. And now he understood how Freddie had become bewitched by her.

"It would probably be best if we don't speak on political matters, my lady," Sinjin said with a grin.

She smiled at Sinjin. "I can see that you're the peacemaker. No wonder you have a reputation as the great compromiser in Parliament."

"You're rather well informed—for a lady," Alex said.

She bristled. "You did not have to qualify your remark. I should like to be well informed without regard to gender."

Alex directed his attention at her. "I don't know you well enough to determine if I could make that statement without a qualifier."

"I don't know *you* well enough to determine if I can make this statement with certainty, but I do believe you are honest." she said.

The three of them broke into laughter. They kept up a lively banter as they ate their fowl and turnips and washed them down with ale. By the time they finished, Alex walked her to the chamber next to his. "I thought you'd feel safer if you knew Sinjin and I are close—should you need us for any reason. I know it's beastly difficult for a lady to travel without even her maid."

"That's very kind of you. I will own, I was a bit ill at ease about sleeping alone in a strange place."

He took her gloved hand and brushed his lips across it. "I bid you a good night, my lady."

As she strode into her chamber, he said, "Don't forget to lock your door."

His valet, Gates, awaited him and helped him dress for bed. His bed, warmed by the fire blazing nearby, was comforting. Folded up for hours on end in a cramped coach was more exhausting than a punishing workout with Jackson. He went immediately to sleep.

* * *

Because the roads were good and the weather free from rain, they were able to easily cover two-thirds of the journey during the first two days.

Then snow began to fall. Georgiana buried herself beneath the woolen rug. Her hands were so cold, she was forced to forgo reading Lord Chatham's book.

"Would that I could offer a warm fire, my lady," the Duke of Fordham said, an apologetic look on his face.

"A fire would be a very good thing right now, your grace. In fact, I shall console myself with thoughts of standing before the fire at Hartworth House. When do you expect to reach London?"

"If the snow doesn't impede our progress—and it's rare when a March snow does—we should arrive at nightfall," Fordham said.

"Your three unmarried sisters are there?"

"Yes."

"What about Lady Roxbury?" Lord Slade asked.

The duke grimaced. "I had the painful task of dispatching a black-bordered letter to her the day before we left Gosingham. Would that I could have told her in person."

"I hated it when your sister moved to the far corners of Devon," Georgiana said. Then, almost as an afterthought, she looked up at him. "You were in the Peninsula when she married, were you not?"

"I was."

She shook her head. "It's difficult to imagine a duke as a soldier."

"It's even more difficult for this old soldier to imagine himself a duke. It's not something I ever contemplated."

"But think about it," she teased. "An army officer has much in common with a duke. Do they both not order about vast numbers of men?"

His face transformed, like sunshine after a storm, and he winked. "You do have a point, my lady."

Even though this man had the most to gain from Freddie's death, she was inclined to believe him when he said he'd never wanted to be a duke. His friend Lord Slade had assured her that Fordham was possessed of great character, and Lord Slade *had* known him well since they were young lads. Slade had a reputation in Parliament as a man incapable lying.

Of course, believing the new Duke of Fordham and trusting him were two different matters. This youngest of the Haversham sons was a known rake, a rake who was attracted to the type of women one never displayed in public.

And he was a Whig.

Thinking of the murder prompted her to ask, "How, your grace, do you plan to make inquiries about the possible murderers once we get to London?"

"I shall start at my brother's club."

"But you never go to White's," Lord Slade said.

"I must go where the Tories go."

The features on Lord Slade's face sharpened. "They'll think your allegiance to the Whigs a casualty to your new rank."

"They can think whatever they like. As committed as I am to the Whigs, I'm more committed to finding my brother's killer. But . . ." He paused, his gaze fanning to her, then to Lord Slade. "The fact he was murdered stays with only the three of us."

"What of Wycliff?" Lord Slade asked.

"Four of us," the duke amended.

Lord Slade turned to her and explained. "Since we were lads at Eton, we three—Fordham, Wycliff and I—have shared everything."

She nodded. "I have such a difficult time believing any of those men who came to Freddie's shooting party could be capable of killing a man, a friend," she said. "Surely it's someone else. It's the kind of thing a thief would do." How foolish she was being. There was no evidence to support her statement, but it was painful—and frightening—to think the murderer might be someone she knew or someone from her own privileged class.

"Did you find out if . . . any females gained entry to Gosingham that night?" she asked. If only Mrs. Langston would be the murderer.

"No females came to Gosingham," the duke said. The look Fordham gave her reminded her of stern Miss Masters, her much-feared governess.

"Had I neglected to tell you that nothing was missing? That all the doors at Gosingham were secured that night—as they are every night?"

She bowed her head like a scolded school child.

"I do share you disbelief," Lord Slade said to her. "It's beyond my comprehension that one of the previous duke's friends could possibly have murdered him."

She thought of the coachman, the very one who was up on the box right now. In his grief over his son's death, could he have sought retribution with Freddie? The thought of coming face to face with him terrified her. "There is the coachman," she said in a feeble voice.

The duke glared at her. "I refuse to consider him until all the others have been exonerated. He's served our family all his life."

The wind began to howl, and she gathered the rug closer in hopes it would warm her against this new assault. "Did it ever get this cold when you were in the Peninsula, your grace?" she asked.

"I never saw snow, but I certainly experienced winds much more chilling than this—and we had no carriages to provide relief. Some of my men went without winter coats after they'd been burned by gunpowder in battles."

"And knowing you," Lord Slade said, "you probably gave away your own coat to an injured soldier."

The duke did not deny it. Her admiration for him grew. She recalled seeing a painting of him at the family's London home in which he was dressed in his red Guards' jacket, standing in his shiny black books, snowy white breeches and gleaming sword. How handsome he'd been. And still was.

Fordham eyed her with concern. "You look beastly cold. Should you like my coat? I assure you I'm accustomed to the cold."

She was touched. "It's very kind of you to offer, your grace, but the rug makes the cold tolerable. I do pity your poor coachman—all coachmen, really."

"They are inured to the cold. Rains, I believe, make one more miserable," the duke said.

Lord Slade emitted a mock shiver. "The worst is cold *and* rain."

"And gusty winds," she added.

The men nodded.

"Please," she said with a laugh, "let us speak of roaring fires, cozy inns, or sunny days in Spain— anything but snow and fierce, cold winds!"

"How about Whig politics?" the duke said, a mischievous glint in his mossy coloured eyes, eyes that were so much like Freddie's.

It was really remarkable how closely the two brothers resembled. Both were of muscular build with no great height, though they were considerably taller than she. Without being obvious, she studied him. His light brown-goldish coloured hair must have been blond when he was a youngster. Though it was the same shade as Freddie's, his skin was less fair. Had his tan from the Peninsula last year not faded? Even though both brothers had fine aquiline noses and firm mouths set over a clefted chin, the younger brother's expressions, even though he was in mourning, conveyed a natural playfulness that would have been alien in serious Freddie.

She had to admit the same physical qualities— indeed, handsomeness—that had attracted her to Freddie were present in this rakish brother.

There was something else about him, something she could not put a name to, but it was not difficult to see why females had always thrown themselves at him—so she had been told—even when he had neither rank nor fortune.

"I beg you not discuss Whig politics," she said. "You well know the sympathies of my family—as well as of the man to whom I was betrothed." Her voice cracked on the word *betrothed*.

"We shall make it our mission to convert you, my lady," Lord Slade said, grinning.

The duke directed his attention to her. "How is it you knew that Sin- - , er, Lord Slade was known as the great compromiser if you do not keep up with politics?"

"As you say, your grace, I am well informed . . . for a woman." She could not suppress a smile.

"I mean no disrespect to your gender, but I know of no other woman who follows the goings-on in government," the duke said, then turning to Lord Slade, added, "except for your wife and Wycliff's wife."

She eyed Lord Slade. "I remember reading that you recently married the daughter of Harold Featherstone. Had you met her through her influential father?"

"I had—when her father and I were fellow members of the House of Commons. She was only a girl then, but I was impressed over her knowledge of political philosophy."

"It was much later before he had the good sense to realize Miss Featherstone was his perfect mate," the duke said. "They're both reform mad."

"Then my brother must be your enemy," she said to Lord Slade.

He shrugged. He was far too kindly to disparage

her brother.

"How long have you been married?" she asked.

"Ten weeks."

Her mouth opened in surprise. "Oh, then you're a newlywed. You must miss her dreadfully."

"You don't know how much," he said longingly.

"We fellows—Lord Slade, Lord Wycliff and I— have shared everything, including political philosophy, since we were lads. In fact, we made a pact long ago to be there whenever one of the three of us needed anything." the duke said.

"It's a good thing we did. Otherwise Wycliff— and his beautiful wife—would now be dead."

"Whatever can you be speaking of?" asked Georgiana, her mouth gaping open.

"You remember that business when Lord Tremaine was to be tried in the House of Lords?" Fordham asked.

"I am, after all, well informed." She could not suppress a smile.

"He meant to kill our good friend Lord Wycliff."

"And I take it, you and Lord Slade stopped him?"

He nodded.

The man certainly wasn't one to elaborate upon his accomplishments or his bravery. There were so many questions she wanted to ask, but she did not believe he would want to answer.

It was apparently a subject neither man wished to broach. Lord Slade peered from his window. "The snow's melting when it hits the ground."

By the time they reached Barnet, the roads were free of snow, though the chill still clung to them. The weather did not vary between then and when they reached the Mayfair section of London shortly after nightfall.

First they let off Lord Slade at a slender town house on Halfmoon Street.

Not far away, the coach pulled up to the Fordham mansion on Berkeley Square. As she gazed from the window to see if the upstairs chambers were lighted, she gasped.

His brows dipped. "What's the matter?"

"There are hatchments on your house."

"They already know about Freddie."

$\mathcal{C}$hapter 5

When Alex entered Fordham House, his sister Margaret, her black dress in stark contrast to her pale white skin, was scurrying down the wide staircase beneath a crystal chandelier. She rushed into his arms. He held her close and gently stroked her back as she sobbed into his chest. "I know it's wretched," he murmured.

"How can it be?" she asked in a quivering voice.

He shrugged. He hated not to be completely honest with her, but if he hoped to find Freddie's killer, he couldn't let it be known that he suspected the death was not natural. The murderer must be made to feel he would never be detected. Perhaps that way, the vile man would let something incriminating slip. "Our poor brother died peacefully in his sleep." The statement was substantially true.

Lady Georgiana moved to them and patted her friend's arm. "It could have been that Freddie was born with a defective heart or some such thing." Not an outright lie.

Tears streaking her face, Margaret looked up at Freddie's intended, then moved to embrace her. "Oh, Lady Georgiana, I am so very sorry for you."

"And I'm so very sorry for *you*," Lady Georgiana said, giving her friend a firm hug, then drawing away. "Are your sisters utterly inconsolable?"

"They are, quite naturally, upset." Margaret

swiped away a tear. "And Amelia fancies there's a curse on our family."

"I wondered the same thing," he said. "Where are Fanny and Amelia?"

"They've gone to bed. I do believe Fanny's more upset about having to go into mourning than she is over our brother's death. She was so looking forward to being presented."

"She will be. You ladies can be out of mourning in June. The Season will just be in full swing."

A feeble smile on her face, Margaret nodded. "Thank you, Fordham. I was afraid you'd make us observe the full six months. Then poor Amelia would have to wait another year."

"Three months is a perfectly acceptable period of mourning for a sibling," Lady Georgiana said.

Margaret sighed. "I'm so glad you've come, my lady. You've been constantly in my thoughts." Margaret looked from Lady Georgiana to Alex. "So you two have finally met?"

"I'm afraid I've rather forced my presence upon your brother."

"Not at all," Alex said. He was still stunned that, even her grief, Margaret had so smoothly addressed him by his new ducal title.

Margaret moved to him again and rested her curved fingers upon his sleeve. "You've buried our brother?"

He nodded solemnly.

"Next to Richard?"

"I thought that's where he'd want to be."

"Yes, I think he would." Margaret turned to Lady Georgiana. "This is so dreadful for you—just as you had finally settled on a wedding date."

Lady Georgiana nodded solemnly. "I feel beastly I couldn't have wed him last year. He was such a domestic creature. Two weeks and we would have been man and wife."

Alex remembered the solicitor saying he'd been drawing up Freddie's marriage contracts, but Alex wasn't aware the wedding would have taken place at so soon a date.

"Yes, Freddie was far more suited to be a farmer than a duke," Margaret said with a fragile laugh. "And once he found his perfect mate, all he wanted was to settle down with you." Margaret's voice cracked.

"I beg that you not dwell on the sadness," Lady Georgiana said. "Freddie wouldn't have wanted it. What's done cannot be undone."

Once again, his brother's intended appeared unaffected by the death of her betrothed. The woman was a paradox.

Margaret took the lady's hand. "You are a comfort. Will you stay with us? Please? No need to open up Hartworth House."

Lady Georgiana patted his sister's hand. "I will tonight. We *are* very weary. But tomorrow I must go to our house. My mother's coming, so I must see that the house will be ready for her. As she's not quite up to managing stairs, I'm going to have the servants move her furnishings into the morning room on the ground floor." She sighed. "I ought to force her to climb stairs. Even though she doesn't believe so, I know she's capable."

The paradox again. Soft and hard, like stone and sable. Still, he was indebted to her. She had raced off to London with him, with no regard for her feminine needs. And her presence had been comforting to Margaret. He suspected his other sisters, too, would be cheered by her. She did have a way of pushing aside her own grief in the most pragmatic manner.

* * *

They all met for breakfast in the dinner room, where the sideboard had been laid with breakfast offerings. Georgiana had listened for footsteps in the corridor before making her way downstairs. She was the last to arrive in the sunny saffron-coloured chamber.

Amelia's face brightened. "I did not know you were here, Lady Georgiana! What a pleasant surprise." She rose to come embrace her.

"Why are you not wearing black?" asked Fanny, who stayed seated and glared from beneath lowered brows at her dead brother's fiancée.

Georgiana squeezed Amelia then came to drop a kiss on Fanny's head. "I have not been home since . . . I rushed to see Freddie before he was buried." She poured herself a cup of coffee and placed a piece of toast on a small porcelain plate that bore the Duke of Fordham's crest of a three-tailed lion.

The duke indicated for Georgiana to take a seat between him and Margaret. The five of them gathered around at one end of the long mahogany table. "Lady Georgiana had not a care for her own possessions. She fled with me to London in order to offer you comfort when I broke the sad news to you. We didn't know you'd already heard of Freddie's death."

Georgiana's brows lowered. "How did the sorrowful news reach you so quickly?"

"I bumped into our solicitor's clerk on The Strand, and—not knowing we hadn't heard the horrifying news—he offered condolences."

Georgiana's hopes that the murderer had tipped his hand were dashed.

Margaret set down her cup of tea and smiled at Georgiana. "It was very kind of you to come to us."

"Little did I know when Lady Roxbury became my dearest friend the year we came out that her sisters would become as dear to me as she is," Georgiana said.

"We're all so fortunate to have you for our friend, my lady." Amelia said.

Fanny's mouth gaped open. "Did you really come all the way to London without a single portmanteau?"

"A very small valise for the night at Gosingham," Georgiana said. "That should explain why I look so appalling."

"You could never look appalling." Amelia then flicked her gaze to her brother. "Do you not agree, Fordham?"

His brooding gaze moved to Georgiana and studied her for a moment. Her cheeks heated, her heartbeat roared. How embarrassed she was to have merited such perusal when she could not have looked worse. She unconsciously started combing her fingers through her disheveled hair, wishing like the devil Angelique had come, wishing she had worn a pretty, freshly ironed dress instead of the faded sprigged muslin she'd worn every other day that week.

"You do not look appalling," said he.

Which made her feel even worse. Any other gentleman would have told her she was pretty— even if it were a lie. Through narrowed eyes she watched as he proceeded to eat the first of two eggs.

Fanny tried to smooth over the awkwardness. "It was very kind of you to come, my lady." We've had a bit of time to let Freddie's death sink in, so we're not the watering pots we were when we heard two days ago."

"For which I am most thankful," the duke said.

Margaret eyed her brother. "I mean no disrespect to Freddie or his memory, but I've always believed you were the brother who would make the best duke." Her eyes moistened.

Georgiana wasn't sure, but she thought the duke also blinked away tears. How sad that of the three brothers, there was only one left.

"You say that because you and I are closest in age, and I've always been your favorite brother."

"While I cannot deny that you always were my favorite, I firmly believe you're possessed of greater leadership capabilities than either Freddie or Richard, and just look at your exemplary military career—and all you've accomplished in Parliament in so short a time."

He smiled. "Lady Georgiana has commented that my role as an officer ordering around vast numbers of soldiers should prepare me for my ducal role of ordering around a vast number of servants."

The all laughed. Which was very good.

"Seriously," he said, gazing at Margaret, "being a duke is not a title I ever wanted. I was happy to be a duke's third-born son." His gaze swept over the gathering. "But I vow to do my best. I shall endeavor to be a capable steward of our ancient family and its properties."

"And," Fanny said, "don't dwell on regrets that you and Freddie weren't close. He knew you loved him, and in his own . . . cold way, he loved you. I remember how Mama used to despair when the two of you came to fisticuffs as young lads. She feared one of you would kill the other."

Those words chilled Georgiana. *One of you would kill the other.*

"All brothers go through that phase," Margaret countered, shooting a scolding look at her youngest sister.

This was the first Georgiana had heard of angry fights between the two brothers, and the first time she'd heard Freddie described as cold. He'd not been cold to her, but now that she considered it, iciness *did* describe his demeanor with others.

The door to the room opened, and in the doorway stood the butler, along with a handsome, dark-haired man who looked to be the same age as the duke. He was accompanied by a beautiful blonde woman who was likely the same age as Georgiana. Was this man Fordham's other great friend, Lord Wycliff? Only very close friends could enter a chamber without having previously been announced.

Fordham stood and moved to the newcomers.

"I am so sorry about your brother," the man said, coming to splay one hand on his friend's back. "We both are."

The blonde, beautifully dressed in a rose-coloured morning dress with matching pelisse and cap, joined them and in a soft voice offered her condolences.

When the man eyed Georgiana, the duke intervened. "Lord Wycliff, I should like to present Lady Georgiana Fenton."

Lord Wycliff bowed. "Were you not the late duke's intended?"

"Yes," Georgiana said solemnly.

"Then I'm very sorry for your loss."

"Thank you."

"I should like to present my wife to you."

Georgiana and Lady Wycliff offered each other a feeble smile and murmured greetings.

Lady Margaret addressed her brother. "Lord Wycliff called yesterday to console you."

Lord Wycliff nodded. "Jane Slade told me you and Sinjin had gone to Gosingham before your brother's death."

The duke nodded. "Beastly of me to take him away from his bride, but we needed what I thought would be Gosingham's solitude to work on the penal reform bill. We'd have asked you were you not already knee-deep drafting your speech on the matter."

Lord Wycliff nodded. "Would that I were possessed of the talent for delivering unprepared eloquent speeches."

"Ah, like the genius of Charles James Fox."

"You *are* eloquent, my dearest," his wife said. Then she directed her attention at the duke.

"I am only barely accustomed to calling my dear friend Jane Slade, instead of Jane Featherstone, and now I shall have to become accustomed to calling you Fordham."

The lady must be trying to put a more cheerful bent to a sad occasion.

How convenient, thought Georgiana, that two such good friends, Lord Wycliff and Lord Slade, had married women who were already good friends.

The beautiful countess turned to Georgiana. "How long will you be in London, my lady?"

"I expect to be here for several weeks."

"Jane Slade and I would be honored if you'd attend our Tuesday gatherings. My husband calls them bluestocking meetings," Lady Wycliff said with a good-natured smile. "We're all reform mad."

"Then the meetings are political?" Georgiana asked.

"Oh, yes."

"Then I must decline."

The blonde's face fell. "You're sympathetic to the Tories?"

Georgiana nodded.

"I would wager my wife will do her best to convert you, Lady Georgiana."

"I will be flattered if Lady Wycliff honors me with her attentions."

Lord Wycliff's attention returned to his friend. "Sorry to barge in on your breakfast, old fellow. We wanted to come before I have to go to Parliament."

The duke gave a false chuckle. "Now all three of us will be in the House of Lords."

"And after we worked so hard to win your seat in the House of Commons," Lady Wycliff said.

"I hope to sponsor your brother-in-law in the by-election, my lady," Fordham said.

Her face brightened. "Edward Coke?"

"Yes."

"Oh, that would be wonderful! I must go tell Ellie." She slipped her arm through her husband's, and they bid farewell.

Even if the woman was a reform-mad Whig sympathizer, Georgiana took an instant liking to her. There was a sincere warmth about her.

The Duke of Fordham was another matter. Georgiana kept wavering on her opinion of him. She wanted to be unbiased in her judgment. It was true that not only did Lord Slade speak so glowingly of him, but so did the Haversham sisters, the former having known him since the age of seven, the latter all of their lives. Yet

Freddie's relationship with his only living brother had been strained. Freddie never spoke glowingly of him.

And the new duke was the only person to substantially profit from Freddie's death.

She couldn't dispel the words Fanny had said. The late duchess had feared her youngest son could kill Freddie. Or vice versa.

$\mathcal{C}$hapter 6

The Hartworth House footmen carried down the furnishings from the dowager's bedchamber and reassembled them in the morning room just off the entry hall under the watchful eye of Georgiana, who insisted on instructing in the placement of every item. She was grateful the morning room was the most sparsely furnished chamber in their town house. Its only contents were a half a dozen side chairs, a slender secretary, and a card table, which she ordered the servants to carry to the dowager marchioness's chamber.

A pity nothing could be done at present about the scarlet draperies at the pair of windows which looked out over Cavendish Square. Mama's bed curtains and coverlet were of a Sevrés pink. They did not go well together. Since Mama was a great deal more interested in aesthetics than her daughter, she was sure to express her dissatisfaction in a most verbal manner.

Would it be too great an extravagance to commission new pink silk draperies for what Georgiana hoped was a short period of time? Just when she was on the brink of summoning the drapers, she changed her mind. It would do Mama good *not* to admire her new chambers. Perhaps then she would toss away that cane, climb the stairs as she once did, and order the restoration of her old room.

It was late that afternoon when the duke called—surprising Georgiana greatly. She had the distinct impression he had been glad to be rid of her after five straight days in her presence. When Roberts showed him into the former morning room, she looked up to see the Duke of Fordham filling the doorway. He was not a big man like Lord Slade, who was very large, but his deeply muscled body most admirably bespoke supreme masculine strength. It occurred to her this man *was* born to be a duke. The strength of his character had never faltered for a single moment these past several trying days. It took no effort to imagine how effective he must have been as a military officer.

"Your grace, what a pleasant surprise."

"I thought I'd apprise you that two trunks of Freddie's papers have arrived, and I took the liberty of delivering them here. Where would you like them?"

These were in addition to the two valises she already had. "Two trunks?"

He nodded.

She blew out a breath. "That's more than I was expecting." She thought for a moment. "Since it will be some time before we're up for entertaining, let's put them on the dining table. I fancy I'll be arranging them into categories, and that long table will give me much room."

He instructed his servants to bring in the trunks.

She looked up at the duke. "Would you be interested in seeing Freddie's papers? I suppose you're the rightful owner of them. I'm just the organizer."

"You're much more than that. Freddie was counting on you to make decisions on what was worthy of keeping and what should be tossed into the fire. I do thank you for asking me. I should like to see if he kept any of my letters—and also anything that might shed light on his death."

She nodded. "Can you stay now? I've just finished here and shall positively wither away from boredom." She looked down at her wrinkled dress. "As you can see, I can hardly go out in public as I now look."

He smiled. "I *would* advise against going out."

"You, your grace, are most UNgallant."

"Then I must redeem myself by attempting to banish your boredom."

She smiled as she swept from the room, leading him to the dinner room. It took both of them emptying papers and correspondence for fifteen minutes before the trunks were empty and mountains of paper stacked the length of the twenty-foot table.

"I do not envy you your task, my lady."

"Perhaps you'd like to come back after I've sorted this mess?"

"I can't leave all of this with you. Like you, I have nothing else to do at present, and it will help pass the time. Closer to dark I'll go to White's."

She pouted. "How I wish I could."

She spied a packet of letters written in a most feminine hand. Were they from Mrs. Langston? She plucked them from the stack, peeking inside to see the signature, and started a new pile. "Hmmm. *Not* from Mrs. Langston."

"He *was* thirty. There were others before he fell in love with you." The duke came closer to the table. "Were you planning to start reading now or just sort?"

"I'm only reading to find the sender's name so that I *can* sort. When I start reading, I should like to start with women's correspondence."

He gave her a surprised look. "I should have thought you'd begin with correspondence from the five men of the shooting party."

She glared at him. "Seven."

"But Lord Slade and I were not of the shooting party."

"But you were in the house that night, and you are suspects."

He stared at her through narrowed eyes. No words were needed. The iciness of his gaze superseded any words he could have uttered.

Finally, she gathered her wits. "Of course you're right about how I should prioritize the correspondence. We must first read all correspondence from anyone who slept at Gosingham that night. I was swayed by feminine sensibilities—which I will own, is unusual for me."

"Any deviation from normalcy is understandable under these grievous circumstances."

After a few minutes of sorting, she asked, "Would you know the handwriting of any of those men?"

He shrugged. "Only my cousin Robert Cecil's. I'll look for his and mine."

She wondered if the duke had removed any of his letters before bringing them here. Did he have something to hide?

"We should both recognize the handwriting from each of your sisters. I expect quite a few letters will be from them. Let's just put theirs back in the trunks—a stack for each sister. Do you think they'd like their letters returned?"

"Ask them."

In the next few minutes, she and the duke contributed to the growing stacks in the trunks. "At least that's helping us clear out a sizeable portion of the correspondence," she said. "I see no reason for me to even think of reading their letters. Do you?"

"No." Brows lowered, he took a folded correspondence from a towering stack and read the signature. "From my cousin. Where should you have me put it?"

"Let me see. I came across one of his." She pointed to the opposite side the table. "Here."

"Does your family, like ours, have archives going back for centuries?" she asked a moment later.

"Oh, yes."

"As the reigning head of the family you should familiarize yourself with some of it."

He paused to glare at her. "You're right—though I've never had a desire to do so."

"It's quite interesting to see, for example, the logs that list all the servants and how much things like candles or even fillies cost two hundred years ago," she said.

He continued sorting. "Don't tell me you actually seek out those old papers?"

"I'm fascinated by them."

"That explains why Freddie chose you for this thankless task."

It was true that Freddie did know quite a lot about her, though she never felt she knew a great deal about him. Since her mother's decline, she had made it a point to write to her betrothed every day, filling the pages with enumerating the mundane events of her day. Many of those days she had spent poking about in the Fenton family archives.

"Oh, look here," she said. "It's the receipt for the Raphael he purchased a few months ago. I had no notion he paid *that* much for it!" She turned to him. "You must now be an exceedingly wealthy man."

"I'm much more interested in finding Freddie's killer than in learning the extent of my wealth."

Since she had kept moving down the table, she found herself next to him. He looked down at her. "I didn't realize how small you are," he said.

She was not only slightly shorter than the average woman, she was also far more slender than she would have liked. "You're not the first to make such an observation. I think it's because, as the first born in my family, I've always had a somewhat authoritarian personality that makes me seem . . . larger."

"So you, too, are accustomed to ordering about a vast number of people."

She looked up at him and smiled. "I suppose we do have that in common."

She moved to the other side of the table, and they continued their sorting for the next two hours while keeping each other apprised of what stacks were being created. There was a fairly high stack of his own correspondence to his brother, but it was by no means complete.

At six, he took his leave in order to go home to dress for dining at White's. "May I return tomorrow?" he asked.

"Please do. I'll be anxious to hear if you learned anything at Freddie's club."

* * *

Shortly after Alex arrived back at Fordham House, Freddie's best friend called. Alex was half way through getting dressed when Mannings announced him. "Show him to the library. I'll be right down."

When Alex strolled into the darkened library, he didn't see Lord Pomfoy at first. The small chamber was lighted only from the fire. Pomfoy rose. "Your grace, I've come to offer my . . ." The man could not finish for he broke into tears, shaking his head and burying his face in his hands. "I can't believe your brother's gone," he managed in anguished sobs.

Alex moved to him and set a gentle hand on the man's heaving shoulders. It was a sad reflection on his closeness to his brother that Pomfoy's grief exceeded his own. "Pray, come sit by the fire. I'd like to talk to you since you were one of the last persons to see Freddie alive."

Nodding, Pomfoy sniffed and came to sit on an asparagus-coloured sofa in front of the fire.

Alex poured two glasses of Madeira, handed one to Freddie's greatest friend, and came to sit beside him. "What can you tell me about Freddie's last day?" Even though Alex and Sinjin had been under the same roof, they hadn't seen Freddie or his friends that day. His and Sinjin's dinner was brought to the library on a tray so they wouldn't have to impede the progress they were making drafting the bill.

"Then it's true? He died in his sleep our last night at Gosingham Hall? My God, I was right across the corridor from him!"

"And you heard no noises coming from his bedchamber? No sounds that awakened you?"

"No, nothing. I'm afraid we all had too much to

drink. We went to bed fairly early—the combination of heavy drinking and having had to get up so wretchedly early to shoot."

"Then Freddie was foxed?"

"He was—but not so much that the spirits would have killed him. He drank no more than I."

Alex nodded.

"He seemed so happy," Pomfoy said, shaking his head. "He'd bagged more than any of us that day, and he was greatly looking forward to marrying and having Lady Georgiana come to live at Gosingham. You know what an old country soul he was. When we were alone he told me how much he was looking forward to starting a family. He wanted a lad to teach how to ride and shoot."

Yes, that was Freddie. While other dukes and noblemen were taking their places in Parliament and involved in ruling the country, Freddie was content to roam about his lands, stripping them of living creatures.

Alex needed to ask more questions without giving away his suspicions. "I wonder if something was oppressing him enough to cause a fatal heart attack. Had he had any kind of disagreements with any of those in your shooting party?"

"Not at all. Everyone was quite jolly. Hence the sottishness of the lot of us."

"It's rare to get a group of inebriated men together and not have one who turns mean."

Pomfoy puckered his lips in thought. "He wasn't actually mean, but Sir Arthur was clearly jealous of Freddie having been Mrs. Langston's protector before him. I do believe Sir Arthur fancies himself in love with the actress."

Alex's attention peaked. "What kinds of things did he say?"

"Only that the actress was frequently bringing up Freddie and Freddie's generosity to her. Sir Arthur's pockets aren't nearly so deep as Freddie's. It seems the woman continued wearing a diamond bracelet Freddie had given her and delighted in flaunting it. Sir Arthur asked her not to wear it, and the lady refused." Pomfoy swigged his brandy. "Once Sir Arthur was in his cups, he cursed Freddie over the bloody bracelet."

It sounded as if Sir Arthur resented Freddie. But enough to want to remove him permanently? "It's all beastly," Alex said. "I know you and Freddie have been close since you were at Eton."

"The two of us were rather forced to band together. We were smaller and less athletic than the others, and we were rather picked upon all our years at Eton. Thank God we had each other. I don't know what I shall do now. Freddie was my only friend." Pomfoy's voice cracked.

"You're no longer a boy at Eton." Alex placed a hand on the other man's shoulder. "You're a grown man. A viscount. Everyone finds you admirable." A pity his growth hadn't kept pace with Freddie's. Pomfoy's size was closer to that of a sixteen-year-old youth than a man of thirty.

One suspect was exonerated. Alex was convinced that Pomfoy would never have taken Freddie's life.

* * *

His father and both his elder brothers had been members at White's, but Alex had rarely gone there. Most of his adult life had been spent fighting in the Peninsula, and since he returned, he'd spent more time at Brook's because Sinjin and Wycliff preferred it—as did most Whigs.

He'd asked Wycliff to accompany him there this

night. During the coach ride he'd shocked his friend by revealing his suspicion that Freddie had been murdered. He told Wycliff about the shooting party and that he believed one of them must be responsible for Freddie's death.

As the coach pulled up in front of the narrow white stone building on St. James, Wycliff said, "So we're hoping some of those men who were in the shooting party are here tonight?"

Alex nodded.

"It's not as if any of them are going to say, *sorry, old fellow, but I suffocated your brother,*" Wycliff said.

Alex turned back from disembarking and glared. "I don't know what it is I'm looking for, but I feel that if I'm around them enough, there will be some kind of sign."

Inside, Alex scanned the chambers for any members of the shooting party—at least the ones he knew. Under his breath, he asked, "Do you know Lord Hickington?"

Wycliff shook his head. "Don't forget I was out of the country as many years as you."

"Oh, yes. Off *making* your fortune." *Stealing—* but only from the despised French. At least Wycliff was redeeming himself now in service to their country.

Not recognizing any members of the shooting party, the two men went into the dining room and sat at a long table where some dozen men had already assembled. Wycliff nodded to several who were in the House of Lords with him.

When they recognized Alex, one and all offered condolences on Freddie's death. How in the devil had so many in London learned? Alex exchanged greetings with several men he'd gotten to know in the House of Commons.

"I suppose there will be a by-election for your seat in the House of Commons now," Anthony Chilton said. "Any idea who might be standing for the office?"

"Yes, Wycliff's cousin, who's also his brother-in-law, Edward Coke."

"Fine man," Chilton said.

A man who appeared to be a half a dozen years Alex's senior and who sat at the far end of the table from him, nodded to Alex. "Your grace, I particularly want to let you know how stricken are all your brother's friends over his death. I was of his shooting party and must have been one of the last people to ever see him alive."

This man must be Hickington. "And you are?"

"Lord Hickington."

"Pray, my lord," Alex said, "could I impose on you to move down here by me? I should be most grateful if you could tell me about my brother's final days."

"Of course, your grace."

The man picked up his plate and utensils, and a footman rushed to carry his wine glass.

"I doubt I have anything interesting to tell you," he told Alex as he took a seat near him.

"I understand most of you were foxed that last day."

Hickington chuckled. "That's true."

"What time did my brother retire for the night?"

"I doubt any of us could be certain of the time. It had to be well before midnight. I do remember your brother saying, "I know many of you must leave early in the morning, and as I am normally not a morning person—unless I'm shooting—I shall say my farewells now.""

Alex swallowed. It hurt like the devil that even though he'd been at Gosingham, he'd not been able to say farewell to his brother.

"Thank God we all expressed our gratitude to him for hosting the party," Hickington continued. "We'd had a great good time."

Even though Alex knew his brother had been in excellent health, he had to justify his volley of questions. "How did my brother look? Did he see in good spirits? In good health?"

Hickington shrugged. "Remember, your grace, none of us were in a state to observe well, but I'm sure the late duke seemed quite healthy."

"And you heard no noises in the night?"

"No."

"Where was your bedchamber?"

"I was on the same side of the corridor as your brother. First your brother's room, then Sir Arthur's, then mine."

So Sir Arthur was next to Freddie. This definitely bore investigating.

"Speaking of Sir Arthur, did he and my brother seem to be on friendly terms?"

"When sober, yes. But after the baronet got deep in his cups, he became, I thought, belligerent to his host. Why do you ask?"

Alex shrugged. "I just wondered if something could have upset Freddie enough to bring on a heart attack or some such fatal malady. That's all."

Hickington shook his head gravely. "It's such a melancholy affair. Poor Fordham. So young. We are all, quite naturally, grievously upset."

"Yes. All his family are."

"What of Lady Georgiana?" Hickington asked.

Alex blew out a breath. "I had the unenviable

task of telling her. Thankfully, the lady did not display the waterworks I'd dreaded."

"She is a most singular lady, to be sure."

It was then that Alex recalled the acquaintance between the lady and this man. "Though she's distressed, she was most anxious to assist me when breaking the sad news to our sisters."

"So she's in London?"

"Yes."

"I must call on her."

"She's not seeing callers yet. Her trunks have not arrived."

Hickington's brows dipped. "Did she accompany you to London?"

Was the man eager to malign Lady Georgiana's character? Alex glared at him for a moment before he responded. "She accompanied me—and Lord Slade." After that, he had no more questions for Hickington, who proved to be the only member of Freddie's shooting party to come to White's that night.

Later, while riding home, he and Wycliff discussed the suspects. "I cannot imagine any possible motive for Lord Hickington to want to kill your brother," Wycliff said.

"I know."

Before Wycliff left the carriage, Alex said, "Not even my sisters have been told about the suffocation. Everyone is to think Freddie died of natural causes."

$\mathcal{C}$hapter 7

Oh, how Georgiana wished Angelique were in London! It had become vastly unpleasant to wear the same two dresses day in and day out—especially without washing them. Georgiana even contemplated trying her hand at washing one, but such a skill was completely beyond her realm of experience.

She rather fancied she did possess the skills necessary to survey and catalogue the contents of the two bulging trunks of Freddie's papers. Doing so had kept her up until three this morning, and she still lacked any sense of accomplishment. All she'd managed to do was to scan a document long enough to ascertain the subject and the sender and to attempt to sort it accordingly.

Lack of table surface for all the categories, though, proved a problem. She resorted to combining various senders together. There were piles for each member of the shooting party, a stack for Mrs. Langston, and Freddie's sisters' letters now reposed in stacks in the two trunks. Tradesmen's accounts were sorted by subject.

Though she would never admit it to anyone, she was inordinately curious about matters she had no right to be—reading letters from the actress who'd been Freddie's mistress. It took tremendous discipline on Georgiana's part not to have read them already.

Hands on her hips, she stood gazing along the expansive dinner table, wondering what would be the best method to permanently save all these piles. Poor Freddie. He wouldn't like his papers left unguarded so higgledy-piggledy for even the servants to see.

The door opened, and Roberts announced the Duke of Fordham.

It was not yet noon! He was *not* behaving very dukishly. Didn't he know that dukes never rose at so early an hour? And he not only was awake, but he was also dressed and presumably fed and was paying calls! His habits must have been shaped by his years as an officer in the Peninsula. "Oh, dear. Do have him come here."

Her first errant thought was another lament that she had no Angelique to render her more attractive. Which was a hideously hedonistic thing to ponder under such grave circumstances. She really was a terrible person. Freddie was better off dead than married to one as insensitive as she.

A moment later the duke entered the sunny chamber, his gaze traveling over the length of the mahogany table before greeting her. "Have you even slept?" he asked.

"Not a great deal. I was unable to pull myself away until sometime this morning. Then when I went to bed, my mind would not oblige. It kept thinking of ways to better organize these papers."

"I understand why Freddie wanted you for this commission, but I'm certain he wouldn't have wanted you to lose sleep over it."

She shrugged. "You have discovered my deplorable single-mindedness. Of course, your brother was too well aware of my silly obsessions."

"You make your . . . talents sound like vices

when they're far from it."

"You are much too kind, your grace." She shrugged. "Enough about me. I'm eager to hear what you might have learned at White's last night. Should you like to sit down?"

He grinned. "What? And have you sitting there thinking of all you could be accomplishing with your mounds of papers if you didn't have to entertain me?"

How could this man have come to understand her so thoroughly in so short a time? It was almost as if he were reading her mind. Even as he'd spoken, she'd been unfolding a letter to see the signature. She laughed. "By the way, your grace, the letters you wrote to your brother repose on the sideboard. I've found quite a few more."

He strolled to the sideboard, eyed them, and nodded. "At least he kept them. I wondered if he destroyed them whenever he was out of charity with me."

"Brothers may have spats with one another—my brothers certainly do—but deep down they love each other. I know Freddie loved you." A slight prevarication. Freddie only discussed his youngest brother when he *was* out of charity with him. "Do tell me about White's last night."

"There's not much to tell. The only member of the shooting party there was Hickington—upon whom I forced my acquaintance. I asked him a great many questions, and he was most obliging. I did learn that Sir Arthur was in the chamber next to Freddie. I suppose I could have learned from the housekeeper where each guest was that night, but proximity has little relevance."

"True. Any person in the house that night had equal opportunity to steal into Freddie's chamber after everyone had gone to sleep. By the way, did you ever speak to Freddie's valet?"

"Yes."

"Was it your brother's custom to lock his bedchamber door?" she asked.

"He said since Freddie had so many servants coming and going and since the house itself was locked every night, Freddie never locked his door."

"I wonder if his friends knew this."

"I wondered the same thing," he said. "I've been told from two sources that all the fellows were heavily in their cups that night."

She stared coldly at him. "Since you were there, I should have thought you'd already know that."

"But I never saw Freddie or his guests. Lord Slade and I were there to draft a bill, and we only left the library to go to our beds. We'd arrived that afternoon whilst Freddie was out shooting. You must know how vast Gosingham is with nearly three-hundred chambers. I never even heard another voice."

"When did you go to bed?"

"We worked in the library until midnight—considerably after members of the shooting party retired."

"And I'd guess those in the shooting party went into a sound sleep as soon as they laid upon their beds." Her brows rose. "But, of course, since this was a premeditated murder, the killer must have faked being bosky."

"Good point."

She was still distressed that one of Freddie's guests—or his brother—could have killed him. Her stomach went queasy, her pulse accelerated, and the idea of being in the same chamber with any of them now sent a bolt of fear through her. "I don't think I can tolerate being in the presence of any of them."

He shot her a sympathetic gaze. "Hickington wished to pay you a call to offer his condolences. I told him you weren't receiving callers as your trunks hadn't arrived. I . . . did have to apprise him of the fact you came to London with me—and Lord Slade. Since Lord Slade's character is unimpeachable, his presence should protect your reputation."

"I have little thought for my own character. Now that Freddie's dead, I cannot imagine marrying, and if I did, most gentlemen could ignore a bit of tarnish to get their hands on my dowry."

"Even with no dowry, you would have no difficulty capturing a man's heart. I do believe you're the only woman Freddie ever fell in love with, and he had a large field from which to choose."

An amused expression on her face, she turned to him. "Pray, your grace, besides my dowry and my rank, do you really find I have *attributes*?" Now why had she gone and asked such a coy question? Given this man's previous honesty with her, she fully expected him to embarrass her with brutal frankness.

His gaze met hers then lazily travelled the length of her body. Her cheeks grew hot. There was something seductive about the way he so slowly regarded her. When he finally looked up, his eyes were hooded and his voice husky. "Men will find you lovely."

She was speechless. His words were like a caress. She felt as if her heart were expanding out of her chest. How could this man who had obviously held her in disfavor speak so . . . so admiringly?

Clearly, she must redirect the conversation before she turned into a heap of porridge. "You've never been more kind, your grace. Now . . . how can I keep from having to be near any of those wretched men?"

"I could try to put the word out at White's. I feel as if I'm duty bound to protect you—for Freddie's sake."

Perhaps she just *might* melt into that heap of porridge. "I declare, your grace, you are robbing me of breath with your uncharacteristic gallantry. I am most appreciative." Why this sudden kindness toward her? Was it possible he was responsible for Freddie's death and was trying to divert her suspicions away from him?

"I'm not being gallant. I spoke the truth." His gaze fanned over the dining table where unsorted papers still mounted in its center, and smaller, sorted stacks lined the perimeter. "I knew you'd want to know what I learned at White's. Now I need to set in motion plans for the by–election to replace my seat in the House of Commons. If I can be of any service, my lady, you must summon me." He bowed.

She offered her hand, and he brushed his lips to the back of it. Most men of her acquaintance never actually touched her hand with their lips. Unaccountably, she felt that mushy feeling once more. Even fresh from the school room, she'd never experienced such foolish physical reactions to a member of the opposite gender.

Before he reached the door, a volley of voices filled the entry hall. *Mama!* She'd arrived much sooner than expected.

When the dowager saw the duke, she shrieked.

"Merciful heavens! He's risen from the dead!"

Georgiana was quick to intervene. "No, Mama, this is the brother of the late duke." She turned to the new duke. "Your grace, I'd like to present to you my mother, Lady Hartworth."

He bowed, kissed the dowager's hand, and spoke to the older woman with great civility. Lady Hartworth, in turn, responded most favorably, fluttering lashes over sparkling blue eyes.

"His grace has been most helpful to me," Georgiana explained. "You know the late duke made me the custodian of his papers." She waved her hand toward the dining table.

"Dear me, that's a vast amount of papers for one who died so young! I don't envy you the task, dearest." Lady Hartworth turned to the duke. "No one is better qualified than my daughter to perfectly organize your late brother's papers. You will learn that in addition to beauty, Georgiana's possessed of many extraordinary qualities."

"Mama! I beg you not boast about me. His grace will be sure to stay away from Hartworth House throughout our duration here—and just when he's finally warmed to me."

The dowager's brows lowered. "Why wouldn't he warm to you? Men have always adored you."

Georgiana's eyes narrowed. "We will *not* stay in London if you persist in your effusive praise of me. I am most sincerely embarrassed."

"But, my darling, you could not be so cruel to me. It's been more than a year since I've left stuffy Alsop. You know how I've longed to be here in Paris."

"London, not Paris."

"Oh, dear, did I say Paris? Yes, I believe I did." Lady Hartworth turned to the duke. "Please do not think me in my dotage. I know perfectly well what I mean to say, but since my affliction, the words do not always cooperate."

"I could never think you in your dotage, my lady. It's difficult to believe you're even old enough to be Lady Georgiana's mother."

A smile on her face, the marchioness sighed. "Alas, she *was* my first—and I *was* very young."

"Your stupendous debut is still remarked upon," he said.

Which was true. The legions of men who had been captivated by Mama's beauty were still spoken of in drawing rooms and gentlemen's clubs. Georgiana had always lamented that she did not inherit her mother's fair blonde beauty. The only physical similarity between them was their petite size.

Long before she was stricken with apoplexy, Mama had carelessly milked her delicacy as a monk his piety. Georgiana, on the other hand, eschewed being helpless and thrived as an authoritarian firstborn. Even with Freddie, it was Georgiana who had made all the decisions on when and where they were to be married and what would be the terms of the marriage contracts.

"Your grace is too kind," her mother said with a great deal more fluttering of her lengthy lashes— another physical trait Georgiana had inherited, without the flirtatiousness. "Your . . . wife is a most fortunate woman, to be sure," Lady Hartworth said to the duke.

"Alas, there is no wife, my lady," said he.

To Georgiana's mortification, her mother gleamed, flashing a smug glance at her daughter.

The duke went to leave. Georgiana could not

recall when she had ever been more embarrassed. Mama was most overtly throwing her at the eligible duke.

Georgiana's mother pouted like a small child—a child accustomed to getting her way. "I was so hoping you could stay, your grace."

"You must have many things to see to after your long journey," he said. "And you must be very tired. If you will permit me, I should be honored if I may call on you ladies tomorrow."

Beastly man! Why did he have to behave so graciously?

Her mother only too cheerfully consented.

Once he was gone, Georgiana scolded her mother. "I was serious when I said I will not hesitate to take you back to Alsop if you don't stop trying to force a romance with me on the new Duke of Fordham. It's not something I want, nor is it something he wants, and I am bereft of words to explain how mortified I was over your blatant glorification of me."

"But, dearest, the man's perfect for you."

Georgiana scowled. "No more."

A moment later she told her mother she'd moved her bedchamber to the morning room to spare her stair climbing.

"You really are the most thoughtful daughter." The dowager sighed. "It's some compensation for having a half-wit as a daughter-in-law. And to think . . . she's the one who replaced me as Marchioness of Hartworth!"

For once, Georgiana could not refute her mother's criticism. Her sister-in-law, while not a bad person, truly was in want of a brain. It had become most difficult to live with a woman who made such a great many unsound decisions.

Such a misalliance as her brother had entered into could have been avoided if there had been no pressure for hasty weddings—which were all the fashion. Georgiana was a proponent of long engagements to give the couple enough time to know if they were compatible. Marriage was too important a sacrament to sentence oneself to a lifetime with a fool.

She took her mother's slender arm and led her toward the former morning room. The moment they entered the chamber Lady Hartworth frowned. "The draperies must be replaced! Look how they clash with my lovely pink."

"They will not be replaced. Our goal is to get you back in your own bedchamber, to restore your ability to climb stairs."

The dowager shook her head. "I daresay those days are behind me. I could fall and break my hip or other bones and then be truly crippled."

"I won't allow you to speak as if you're in your dotage. Just a few months ago you were still in your forties—much too young to capitulate to such infirmities."

Her mother collapsed onto her chaise. "Is anything more exhausting than travelling? The new duke was right. I am tired. I will own, I didn't want him to leave. I have bawled all week that you're not going to be a duchess, and now I have renewed hope."

"Mother! You cannot mean you're already scheming for me to marry! And to Freddie's brother! You're humiliating me. Listen. To. Me. I am not interested in marrying anyone, and I pray you don't forget I'm in mourning. And one more thing—the new Duke of Fordham doesn't even like me!"

"Foolish girl. All men adore you."

"Freddie told me his youngest brother only has eyes for fair complexioned blondes, and I gather from the time I've spent with him, strong women like me annoy him."

"But, my darling, I'm a strong woman, but your father never knew it. I never said, *I am going to do such and such.* Instead, I would lower my lashes and speak in my most helpless voice and say *What do you think I should do, my love?* I always got my way. That's being a strong woman."

"I am cursed with being hopelessly honest. I could never be like you."

"You affront me! I do not lie."

"Forgive me. I did not mean to imply that you're dishonest."

Lady Hartworth sighed. "I only want what's best for my children. I do so worry about Philip, and it's such a pity Hart is married to that horrid woman."

Georgiana, too, worried about her youngest brother, who was an officer in the Peninsula, but she no longer worried about the marquess. "Don't feel badly for Hart. He's happy. He seems to be in love with Hester in spite of her shortcomings, and they adore those children."

Lady Hartworth shuddered. "Rotten children."

"You shouldn't say that. You know you love them."

"How unnatural I would be if I didn't! But it is trying to be around the little hellions."

"I know."

Lady Hartworth closed her eyes. "The late duke was not your husband. You're not required to mourn him."

"I'm not interested in marrying Freddie's

brother—or in marrying anyone." Georgiana stormed to the door.

"But, my darling, Hamford is so much nicer than stiffy stuffy Freddie ever was."

"Fordham, not Hamford."

"Oh, dear, I truly did mean to say Fordham."

$\mathcal{C}$hapter 8

Night had just fallen when Alex paid a call at Hartworth House. He'd not planned on returning until the following day, as he'd promised Lady Hartworth, but since he found himself free of any activity for a the next two hours, he thought to assist Freddie's affianced with her nearly insurmountable task. And, selfishly, he was growing anxious to read the correspondence from members of the shooting party, hopeful of gleaning any possible motive for murdering his brother.

Lady Hartworth's frail constitution had sent her to bed for the night already, so he was shown once more into the dinner chamber where the daughter of the house was busily organizing his brother's papers. When she turned around and smiled at him, he caught his breath. The woman was stunning. Her dark tresses had been stylishly arranged around her lovely face. Had her near-black eyes always been so large, her lashes so lengthy?

His gaze whisked over her appreciatively. So the woman did possess fashionable clothing of impeccable taste! The thin muslin gown matched the rose in her cheeks. He swallowed. Freddie had been a most fortunate man to have won this woman's hand.

Of course, her forceful personality was another

matter altogether. She was void of the feminine helplessness he'd always been attracted to.

"You have disabused me of the notion you care not for appearance, my lady."

She started laughing, those jet eyes of her flashing with mirth. "Most other men would have told me how pretty I now looked."

"I am not most other men."

"Indeed, you are not. You are, after all, a duke—a duke who has, I believe, just delivered to me a back-handed compliment. Now, do tell, to what do I owe the pleasure of your visit."

"To be honest, I wished to gauge your progress, and I'd like to begin reading the correspondence from Freddie's last guests."

"I have made good progress." She waved a hand across the table, which was no longer centered by a mountain range of paper. "While I haven't read a single letter in its entirety, I have read all the signatures. It did speed up things considerably that a large percentage of the letters were written in my own hand."

She pointed to the floor where a huge, basket was crested with letters. "Those are all from me." The basket must have held over three hundred letters. "Never, I am certain, has there been a higher concentration of dullness in one place. The only function of those letters would be as an aid to induce sleep."

He chuckled. He found her ability to poke fun at herself refreshing. "I doubt Freddie would have agreed," he said.

"But—and I mean not to speak ill of the beloved dead—Freddie was a dullard himself."

"I cannot refute your statement." He chuckled again. He felt beastly for laughing at his late brother's boorishness, but as she had put it, Freddie was beloved, even if he was a dullard. It did them both good to be able to laugh in the midst of such fresh grief. Eyeing her with amusement, he shrugged. "Your mother must have been exhausted from her journey, in spite of her claims."

"You were very perceptive about her. And while we're speaking of my mother, I do apologize for the zealous manner in which she rather bludgeoned you with my attributes. Ever since I disappointed her the year of my debut, she's feared I'll be the ultimate embarrassment—a hopeless spinster."

He grinned at her. "I have been given to understand that you received several marriage offers the year of your debut."

She hung her shoulders. "Alas, that's true. I am most spectacularly deficient. I keep finding faults with every man who pays me court."

"Were you holding out for a duke? Is that why you went through half a dozen seasons before getting betrothed?"

Her eyes narrowed, and any sense of levity was gone from her face. "It mattered not to me that Freddie was a duke. I suppose I was just tired of having people murmur behind my back about my lack of a husband, tired of living in a house where I was not its mistress, tired of my mother's constant chastisement."

"So that's why you agreed to marry my brother?"

"And other reasons."

"Love?"

She did not respond for a moment. "Freddie was very much in love."

"And what about you, Georgiana?" Why had he

called her only by her Christian name? It was far too intimate. Had she even noticed?

"I found him most compatible."

"What about love? Were you in love with him?"

"That is no concern of yours."

She hadn't been in love with Freddie. By God, she was a woman without feeling. Except, of course, by all accounts she was completely devoted to her mother. Lady Hartworth likely would not be alive today had her daughter not sacrificed herself to see to her mother's recovery.

They stared at each other until her stiffness uncoiled, and that touch of mirth was back in her voice. She cast a glance at the table piled high with Freddie's papers. "I shall be thrilled to finally be able to read some of these letters. And I must own, I shall be even more delighted not to have to bend over that table a moment longer. I feared my spine would turn into a giant comma."

Shaking his head, he smiled at her. Yes, he could see why Freddie had fallen in love with this amusing little beauty who was anything but retiring. Not at all in Alex's line, of course.

"I don't think we have a place to read in this room," he said.

"You're right. We'll go to the library. The footmen can help us."

Moments later, they were sitting across from each other at the long cherry wood writing table where correspondence from each member of Freddie's shooting party had a square of the table's surface. A fire glowing in the hearth and a tall silver candelabrum upon their table illuminated the darkly paneled room. Because it was not large, the library was an exceedingly cozy room.

Roses. Their scent had him searching for a bouquet before he realized the pleasant fragrance came from the woman who sat across from him.

"Before we begin," she said, "I'd like to know a little about your cousin, Robert Cecil. Since you are presently the last duke—at least, the last sired by your father—I was wondering who would be next in line to the Fordham dukedom—if you don't father a legitimate son?"

How foolish of Alex not to have considered that before. Because his father had no living brothers and had, at the time of his death, three living sons, ducal inheritance outside of his immediate family had never occurred to Alex.

But now the succession was a grave concern. Who *would* inherit if Alex died tomorrow? His heartbeat drummed. His hands sweat. *Robert Cecil.* As the eldest son of Alex's father's deceased brother, Robert *was* a direct male descendant of Alex's paternal grandfather, the fifth Duke of Fordham.

A kind-hearted, jolly fellow a few years older than Alex, Robert could not possibly be capable either of murderous thoughts or most especially of murderous actions. Moreover, one capable of killing Freddie for the title would then have to kill Alex in order to succeed to the dukedom. Even though Alex knew Robert was incapable of murder, the prospect of double murders was a most distressing thought, to be sure. A concerned look swiped across his face.

"I can see by your expression, it's Robert Cecil," she said.

He nodded solemnly. "If you but knew the fellow, you'd know how preposterous such a notion is. He's no murderer. He's an honorable man."

"If you hope to find your brother's killer, you must push aside all opinions and force yourself to examine the facts in a coldly calculated manner. It would be far easier if you didn't know any of those men."

This woman could easily suppress emotions. A more calculated woman he'd never met. "You're right, but I still cannot countenance that my cousin would ever contemplate anything so evil."

She threw up her arms. "Fine. Then let's forget that Freddie was murdered. Let's pretend he died peacefully in his sleep. Then you won't have to deal with any further unpleasantness. Unless, of course, the murderer then decides to kill you in order to become a duke."

This maddening woman ignited anger in him. If she were a man, he would likely have delivered a blow to her face. He'd contemplated storming from the chamber. How dare she insinuate his cousin was a murderer! She even believed Robert could be plotting Alex's murder next. The idea was ludicrous.

In one matter, though, she was right. Alex must not allow himself to be blinded by personal feelings.

As much as he wished to refute her suspicions, he decided to say nothing. He would *show* her the killer was not his cousin. He would start with Sir Arthur's correspondence. It was the shortest stack. The first letter was really more of a note, written to accept Freddie's invitation to the shooting party. Although Alex's instinct was to quickly eye it, then go on to the next, he must be extra conscientious with this. Every word bore scrutiny.

He carefully read Sir Arthur's correspondence. He'd started with this man because he hoped—if one of Freddie's friends had to be the murderer—it was Sir Arthur. It couldn't be Robert or Lord Pomfoy or Lord Barnstaple. Alex had known those three most of his life.

Another advantage to starting with Sir Arthur was that he had only written a handful of letters to Freddie. It wouldn't take long to go through them, even if Alex was carefully reading each word.

After reading the first note, he put it aside. Nothing whatsoever could be found to hint at any conflict between the two men. He looked up at Lady Georgiana. As she read beneath the glow of a dozen candles, he noticed her exceedingly long lashes nearly rested on her cheeks. He'd never before realized how beautiful dark-haired women could be. "What are you reading?"

"Your cousin's correspondence, if you do not object?"

He shook his head. "I warn you, you will not find anything in there that will bear scrutiny. Robert's a simple fellow—who, by the way, is an appalling speller."

She laughed. "Yes, I quickly discovered that. He writes *Remember when we were lads*—which he spells L-A-D-D-Z—*and planned to go to Europe.*" She stopped and showed him how Robert had spelled Europe: U-R-U-P.

"I don't think I'd have figured that one out," he said, grinning at her.

"I'm quite good at it because my brother Philip—who's an officer in the Peninsula—is also a most inept speller. He believes cats are spelled with K's and phaeton with an F. But in many other ways, he's quite brilliant."

"Philip Fenton's your brother?"

Her dark eyes danced. "Yes. Do you know him?"

"Not well. We were posted together at Salamanca for a short while, and he was at Eton when I was there, but he was two or three years younger than me. Fine fellow."

"Thank you. He's very dear to me."

So she did possess a heart.

They returned to perusing Freddie's correspondence. Most of Sir Arthur's notes were impersonal and of no interest—save one:

It is my good fortune, your grace, that you've fallen in love with your beautiful betrothed and are no longer in love with Sophia Langston. How you could have spurned dear Sophia mystifies me. A more beautiful, perfectly amiable woman I've never known. Even after all these months I've been honored to have Sophia under my protection, I am still a man very much besotted.

Though there was nothing in the letter to show any resentment toward Freddie, it did reveal Sir Arthur's deep attachment to Freddie's former mistress.

Within fifteen minutes, Alex had read all the missives from Sir Arthur.

"Oh, your cousin speaks of you in this," she said. "He must be quite fond of you. *I try to write to Alex every week and try to be cheerful, though God knows*—he spelled N-O-Z—*I worry like the devil about him.*"

Alex was touched. Even though Robert was closer in age to Freddie, he and Alex had always been exceedingly fond of each other. Sadly, Alex had been closer to Robert than he was to his own brothers. But Robert was very much like a brother. He'd spent most of his childhood at Gosingham, and Alex's father had always treated his nephew like a son. Alex eyed the lady with mock scorn. "And you believe he's plotting to kill me."

"I never said I thought he was plotting to kill you. I merely said it was a possibility, and after what happened to your brother, you ought not to dismiss any possibility."

"I vow to keep my bedchamber door locked at night." He returned his attention to a new stack of correspondence, this from their neighbor, Lord Barnstaple. How he wished people would always date their letters. There must be nearly a hundred here. Alex had no way of knowing which had been penned recently or which were ten years old. Or did he? Freddie had been a duke less than two years, therefore anything addressed to *Your Grace* would have been written more recently.

It took Alex several minutes to scan each in order to place into two groups, one for those addressed to *His Grace* and one for those to *Freddie.*

She, too, must be sorting for the shuffling and crinkling of her papers drew his attention. "Pray, my lady, whatever are you doing?"

"If I'm to do a proper cataloguing of his papers, I must put them in chronological order. Thank the saints he wasn't ninety years old!"

He shook his head. "Glad I am it's you, not me."

"Lord Harley employed a learned man for several years to catalogue his family's papers."

"Then it's a very good thing Freddie only lived three decades." He frowned, mad at himself. "I didn't mean that the way it sounded."

Her voice softened. "I know. K-N-O-W. You see, I can spell."

He offered her a smile, then he settled back in his chair to read. He read for half an hour before he found anything to draw suspicion. He sat up straight. "Listen to this." He proceeded to read the letter from Lord Barnstaple.

Your Grace,

I will own that I was exceedingly disappointed over your refusal to sell me that small parcel near the river where our lands connect. It's such a small piece of your estate, but to me would make a significant improvement. Even more than my disappointment in your refusal is my hurt at being rejected by the man I have esteemed throughout my life, the man I had considered one of my firmest friends.

"There's more, but it's not of this topic," Alex said.

"You believe he might have killed Freddie in the hopes the new duke would allow him to purchase the parcel?"

"I never said I believed it. It's a possibility, and a certain lady has warned me to be open to all possibilities."

Their eyes met again, and then both broke into smiles.

"This is nothing to smile about, but I agree with you. This is a possibility we cannot ignore. I wonder how long before the man approaches you. If he's that eager, I daresay he won't wait long."

He rose. "We shall have to see." Looking down at Sir Arthur's and Lord Barnstaple's papers, he asked, "Can I help you put these up before I go?"

Her face fell. "No. I need to devise a way of storing these in an orderly fashion." She sighed as she circled the table and came abreast of him. "I suppose you'll go back to White's tonight?"

"Yes."

"How I wish I could be there. I've become most passionate in our pursuit of this vile murderer."

Passionate. Yes, he thought, hard as she could be, this woman might be capable of passion. She just hadn't met the right man. He moved closer to her, his eyes never leaving hers. The firelight danced in her blazing gaze. In that instant a profound desire rushed over him like a roaring tidal wave. He pulled her close and lowered his head to settle his lips upon hers for a scorching kiss.

$\mathcal{C}$hapter 9

Beastly, beastly man! The only time a kiss had ever elicited in Georgiana a response akin to passion—no, not *akin* to passion, most decidedly passion—it had to come from a rake! Upon terminating the (very long) kiss, the profligate man at least had the decency to treat her with a semblance of respect—something she doubted he bestowed on the opera dancers and unfaithful wives with whom he normally shared dalliances.

"Forgive me." His glassy gaze trailed over her. "My actions were unpardonable. I'd best leave." He began to walk away, then turned back. "Will you permit me to call on your mother tomorrow? And to check on your progress, my lady?"

The gall of the man! He acted as nonchalant as one who'd just been introduced to a stranger. How could he be so unaffected by THE kiss when it left every nerve ending in her body aflame?

Her cheeks heated. How wanton she'd been! She could not meet his gaze. For the first time in her life, Georgiana was speechless. Truth be told, she did not trust herself enough to speak without betraying the quiver she knew would be in her voice. Finally, glaring at him, she nodded.

Once he departed, it was impossible to return to Freddie's papers. In those moments she'd been crushed in Fordham's embrace, it was as if a cyclone had erratically reordered her bland life.

How could she even attempt to look at the late duke's correspondence when her breath had been taken away by the scoundrel who was his younger brother? The wicked man had more than made good on the promise of turning her into porridge. She felt as if he could have licked her limp body off the Turkey carpet.

Long after he left, a roaring tremble rolled over her from the top of her head to the tips of her unsteady toes. Her brain, too, had liquefied. She was stunned that she—pragmatic, unemotional, icy Lady Georgiana Fenton—had been so physically enraptured in the odious man's arms. But enraptured she had most certainly been. So hungrily had she enjoyed his kiss, she'd felt an enormous void when he drew away.

Even after her heartbeat was restored to normal, she could concentrate on nothing but that wretched man. In spite of his devastating effect upon her, she made a vow to resist him. She must do so out of respect for Freddie—and respect for herself. No two men could be more dissimilar than he and Freddie. This man was accustomed to toying with women's affections without honorable commitment.

It would be best if she could turn him away completely, but she had not the fortitude to do so. She was too invested in discovering Freddie's murderer. And . . . she did not like admitting it, but she enjoyed having another person with whom to go over Freddie's correspondence and other important papers.

When he came tomorrow, she would scold him and insist that such intimacies never be repeated. But would she even be able to look him in the eye without embarrassment?

For a second night, but for entirely different reasons, she was not able to sleep.

* * *

And he'd thought she was cold! Lady Georgiana Fenton kissed with more ardor than a courtesan. It was as if he'd lifted the cauldron's lid, releasing all those simmering passions she'd long repressed. Her response shocked him almost as much as his own actions had. He could not remember even thinking about kissing the lady, yet out of the blue he'd been overcome with an urge so powerful that he'd drawn her into his arms as naturally and unknowingly as the compulsion to breathe.

How thoroughly satisfied he'd been those moments when his lips pressed to hers, when her slender body pressed against him. All thoughts had been obliterated by a surge of euphoria and potent need. Yet underlying the swirl of emotions, the voice of his conscience emerged, telling him how wrong it was to force himself on his dead brother's betrothed. Just once, he wanted to do the wrong thing. He wanted to peel away her clothing and sink into her.

But Alex had never been able to turn his back on doing what was right.

Leaving her was one of the most difficult things he'd ever done. Long after he left her, he could not purge her from his thoughts. He still felt as if her sweet rose scent clung to him. He'd told his coachman to drive around while he collected himself. He felt like an Etonian rattled by his first kiss.

When he finally made it to White's he was rewarded with the presence of Sir Arthur, whom he vaguely recognized. Sir Arthur might lament his lack of prodigious fortune, but the man dressed exceedingly well in a freshly starched white cravat and shirt, finely tailored black coat and gray pantaloons that had not a single wrinkle. His expanded waist and graying hair gave credence to his four decades. Alex almost felt sorry for Mrs. Langston. Losing a duke—a young, not unattractive one—for a mere baronet of modest means and unremarkable appearance must have been demeaning to the actress who was herself well past the blush of youth.

When Alex had first returned to England after being several years on the Peninsula, he'd met Sir Arthur but had not seen him since. As their gazes connected, the older man effected a frown and began to move across the well-lighted chamber. "Ah, your grace, we friends of your late brother are nearly inconsolable. He was a fine fellow and will be much missed."

"Thank you." Alex eyed an unoccupied card table. "Please, come sit with me. I'd like to know about my brother's last days."

As soon as they were seated, the waiter brought brandy. "There's really not much I can tell you," Sir Arthur said. "I will say your brother seemed to be in perfect good health. His shooting was accurate. In fact, he rather left the rest of us in his dust. Crack shot, that man. I just can't believe he's gone. Don't understand how so fit a young man could just die in his sleep." He looked up at Alex. "Though I daresay your family's cursed. Look at your eldest brother. . ."

Was the man trying to convince him that Freddie's life had been taken away because of some physical malady?

"But my father lived to be seventy," Alex

countered.

Sir Arthur smiled. "Then I pray you take after your sire."

"Would you say you were close to my brother?"

Sir Arthur did not answer for a moment. "I wouldn't say anyone was close to your brother."

"Only one well acquainted with him would know how right you are."

A smile easing across his face, the other man shrugged. "When he was in town—not that terribly often, owing to his preference of the country—he, like me, frequented White's. He knew how vastly I admired Mrs. Langston, and when he became betrothed to Lady Georgiana, he offered to pass Mrs. Langston to me. I have been incredibly beholden to him for the favor. She could have merited a man far my superior in every way."

Alex knew good manners dictated that he deny the man's modest claim, but Alex had never been able to lie. "I'm surprised Mrs. Langston had no say in who was to be her next protector."

"Your brother lubricated my way with a large settlement and a hearty recommendation on my behalf."

Then the baronet must have been most beholden to Freddie. "And the arrangement has been mutually satisfying?" What had gotten into him? Alex had never before asked another man such a prying question. "You don't have to answer. I have no right to ask so personal a question."

"I don't object to answering. On my part it's a most satisfactory arrangement, and Mrs. Langston is never happy without a man in her life—though I've always thought she truly loved the late Duke of Fordham."

And now Sir Arthur's competition had been eliminated.

It was impossible for Alex not to think of Georgiana and compare her to the aging actress. It was like contrasting diamonds to tin. No wonder Freddie had quickly dismissed his mistress after winning the affections of Lady Georgiana Fenton. Alex found his breath growing short at the memory of their shared kiss, and he suddenly became irrationally jealous of his brother. Had she ever kissed Freddie as she'd kissed Alex?

Alex yanked his thoughts away from her. "About my brother's last day. . . Did he seem oppressed about anything? Lethargic? Angry? There must have been something." Alex knew full well none of those things had caused Freddie's death, but he needed to see how Sir Arthur reacted.

"Knowing the late duke, I would say it was a fitting last day. He was in good spirits. His shooting had been most fulfilling, the company was congenial, and the liquor flowed. All of us had a wonderful day. Not much of a night. We'd risen early and drunk too much. I daresay we were in bed by ten o'clock."

"Nothing was said that might have upset my brother? No angry words spoken?"

Sir Arthur's brows lowered. "You don't think he took his own life?"

"No, nothing like that. It appears he died of natural causes." Not exactly a lie. It did *appear* he died of natural causes. "I only wondered if something oppressive could have affected his health. It's so unnatural for one of his age—one in perfectly good health—to expire while sleeping."

"True, though I can think of nothing that could

have made him melancholy. Quite the opposite, actually. He was in very good spirits. He was greatly looking forward to marrying Lady Georgiana."

"Your chamber was next to his, was it not?"

"Yes, I suppose it was."

"And you heard no noises in the night?"

Sir Arthur chuckled. "As much as I drank, I rather fell into my bed and I'm afraid I slept like the dead . . ." He stopped, and stiffened. "Do pardon me for my insensitive comparison."

"No pardon needed." He wanted to gauge Sir Arthur's opinion of Freddie but dare not hint at the suspicious nature of Freddie's death. "Given that Freddie was not one to have close friendships, other than the long-standing one with Pomfoy, would you say you thought of him as a friend?"

"I was flattered to count him as a friend." His bushy eyebrows lowered. "Why do you ask?"

Alex usually avoided lying at all costs, but there was nothing usual about these circumstances. "My brother had a small bequest that each of his friends be bequeathed a bottle of his favorite brandy."

"Ah, but your brother had a fine appreciation of good brandy. I should be honored to receive it, though it would be difficult to drink. It's something I should like to keep to be reminded of Frederick Haversham, the late Duke of Fordham. My friend."

He didn't sound like a man capable of murder.

* * *

Even if she was determined to repel any intimacies with the reigning Duke of Fordham, Georgiana was vain enough to wish to look pretty when in his presence. She had dismissed the first three dresses Angelique had presented. "I believe I'll wear the white one with the tiny purple flowers."

"Oh, mademoiselle, that is my favorite on you. White is so stunning with your dark hair and uncommonly white teeth, and the delicate flowers add to your . . . *la féminité*."

It was as if her maid could tap into her thoughts. How else could Angelique know that on this day Georgiana wished to cast away her careless disregard of appearance and wanted her expected caller to find her lovely? Could Angelique possibly know about the kiss? Could she sense that her mistress was mightily fighting her attraction to her dead fiancé's brother?

Angelique beautifully fashioned her hair into a cascade of ringlets that swept away from her face. It was a much more elaborate style than what Georgiana normally wore during the daytime. As she stared into her looking glass, she was inordinately pleased with her appearance. Because of the flattering dress and stunning hair, she hoped no one would notice the dullness of her eyes from lack of sleep. All because of that wretched man and his wicked kiss!

As her maid was finishing Georgiana's hair, Roberts tapped at her chamber door and informed her that she had a caller. Her heartbeat accelerated. *Fordham.* Then the butler added, "A Lord Hickington."

Her whole demeanor caved. Even though she intended to avoid any intimacies with the duke, she was disappointed he wasn't her caller. She was even more disappointed to have to face Louis Hickington. He was actually one of the reasons she had consented to wed Freddie even though she had not been in love with him. He had once been a most determined suitor. Getting married was the only way she could convince Lord Hickington—and other suitors—of her complete disinterest.

She had hoped that Fordham—as he had vowed to do—might have gotten the opportunity at White's last night to tell Lord Hickington she wasn't receiving callers. Now it was up to her to deliver the annoying man the message in person.

He stood when she entered the drawing room. He was a very fine looking man. She believed him near the same age as the new Fordham heir, about nine and twenty. He was taller than Fordham. Lord Hickington had always been interested in fashion and had a propensity to overdress with bold colours and unforgettable embellishments like chunky jewelry featuring animal heads and cravats of non-traditional colours, like blue. Today he gave a nod to tradition by wearing a white cravat, though the height of his shirt points—hugging his square-cut cheeks—and the elaborate tying of his cravat were anything but traditional.

His expertly cut black hair was all that was fashionable. He moved toward her, regarding her with icy blue eyes. "Allow me, my dear Lady Georgiana, to offer you my deepest sympathy on the death of your betrothed."

She nodded as she extended her gloved hand for him to kiss. Unlike that odious Fordham, this man at least had the decency to *not* actually press his lips to her glove. As he made the motions, she could not help but to think of how every touch of Fordham's unhinged her—and how nothing this man could possibly do would ever unhinge her.

But, then, no man ever had before. Until Alex Haversham, the present Duke of Fordham.

She took a seat on a sofa near the fireplace, and he sat opposite her on a matching sofa. "In spite of your great loss, you're looking beautiful, my lady."

She wondered if he had noticed the tell-tale signs of her missing sleep. If he did, he would attribute it to Freddie—and not to Freddie's rakish brother! "My so-called beauty is not a subject I care to discuss. In fact, I wasn't planning to discuss anything with anyone. I haven't been receiving callers."

"Fordham had said something to that effect, but as you and I are such old friends, I could not stay away when I knew you must be suffering. I am honored that you did not turn me away. I had to come and offer my services to help you in any way possible."

"That's very kind of you, but I need no assistance."

"I shan't want to think of you being mired in grief—not when you've always meant so much to me."

"I'm not mired in grief. I'm kept very busy. You see, the late Duke of Fordham named me as executor of his papers. It's a mammoth task which not only keeps me very busy, but it also keeps my mind off my grief."

"But you need a man to see to your well-being. Hartworth's still at Alsop Hall, is he not?"

"I don't need a man." Least of all her spouse-dominated brother. Besides, Fordham was here. He'd promised to keep the gawkers at bay.

"My dear Lady Georgiana, you haven't changed

one iota. Always so independent. I'm happy you've not changed. I fell in love with that feistiness and everything about you the year you came out, and my feelings have never wavered."

She raised her brows. "Did I not hear of you courting Dorothy Hemmings?" Dorothy Hemmings had been a great heiress of Welsh coal mines. She had since married the Earl of Carley.

"Only after you accepted Fordham's offer. I will own, I was devastated." He sighed. "Alas, my heart was not into the courtship of the coal heiress. I kept pining away for the beautiful daughter of the Marquess of Hartworth."

She cupped her hands to her ears. "I will not listen to such comments. How dare you when my dear Freddie's just been buried."

The man effected a contrite expression. "Forgive me. It's just that my feelings toward you are so violent—and unchanging."

A thump, thump sounded on the corridor outside the drawing room, and Georgiana looked up to see her mother moving toward them, heavily leaning upon her cane.

Lord Hickington stood.

"Mama, may I present to you Lord Hickington. Do you remember him?"

Lady Hartworth gazed at him through squinted eyes. "I do not, but I daresay he's one of those men who used to bring you posies and beg you to marry them—before you became betrothed to the king."

His brows crumpled.

"She means *duke*. You'll recall my mother is recovering from apoplexy."

"I would never have known," he said, smiling at the dowager. "You're as lovely as ever, Lady

Hartworth."

Nodding elegantly, Lady Hartworth preened before turning her attention to her daughter. "I heard a man and came to chaperone. I must scold you for entertaining a man alone in this chamber."

Georgiana's eyes narrowed. "The door was open! And I'm hardly a young maiden who needs to be watched over. I'm four-and-twenty and have absolutely no desire to ruin myself with any man."

Her mother came to sit beside her, then raked her appreciative gaze over the gentleman caller. "You must own, Lord Hawkington is a most handsome man, though I do believe I prefer men with sandy-coloured hair—men like the late Duke of Fordham and his heir."

"Are you discussing the man sitting across from us?" Georgiana inquired.

"Of course. Can you not see how handsome he is?"

"I thank you, my lady, but I am Lord Hickington. Not Hawkington."

"Mama, you must keep your opinions to yourself."

Lady Hartworth sighed. "Then I shall endeavor to be silent."

Her mother was incapable of being silent. Georgiana merely eyed Lord Hickington and shrugged.

"I was just telling your daughter, my lady, that since the marquess, your son, is not here in London, I felt it my duty to offer my services to a young lady constricted by grief."

"I daresay Georgiana would be more constricted by grief if my son were here. As a first born, Georgiana's accustomed to being the one to make decisions and to order others about. She's possessed of a very strong personality. Unlike that son of mine. A pity a female cannot inherit."

"I assure you," Georgiana said, "I wouldn't wish to hold a title like the Countess of Sutherland does. It's more responsibility than I should like. I prefer domination over domestic affairs."

Lady Hartworth nodded with satisfaction. "You see, Lord Hickman, she's still feminine underneath her authoritarian demeanor."

"Hickington," Georgiana corrected.

"Oh, many people call me Hickman," he said.

"I thought, dear Mama, you were going to be silent. You know I dislike you praising me to others."

A martyred expression crossed Lady Hartworth's face. "A pity we aren't Orientals. I understand they hold their elders with reverence and would never criticize them in public."

"I daresay you would not be happy with their practice of binding women's feet so they grow no larger than a biscuit and give them grief until the day they die," Georgiana countered.

Lady Hartworth shrugged. "There's always sedan chairs."

"Which I am very happy you've abandoned. Look how well you're walking now." Her mother had become far too attached to the use of her sedan chair and had to be separated from it not without a great display of tears and pleas.

Roberts came into the chamber. "The Duke of Fordham to see you, Lady Hartworth."

As her mother gleefully told the butler to show in the duke, Georgiana observed that the pleasant expression on Lord Hickington's face blanched at the mention of Fordham.

When Fordham stood surveying the gathering at the door to the drawing room, Georgiana's pulse sped up. What a contrast he was to Lord Hickington. His informal clothing of brown jacket, carelessly tied cream-coloured cravat, buff breeches, and brown boots indicated he had probably ridden over on his horse. She recalled how thoroughly the man admired horses. Yet more than the contrast between overdressed formality and comfortable riding wear, the two men differed in so many other ways. While the viscount had obsessed over purchasing a ring with a lion's head, Fordham had been leading men into battle. Every inch of his muscular torso bespoke of his supreme masculinity.

Then she remembered being held in his arms, and she felt as if every cell in her body tingled.

He strode to her mother and quite correctly kissed the air just above her proffered hand. "You're looking lovely today, my lady."

Lady Hartworth glowed.

Then he turned and in the most proper manner mock kissed Georgiana's hand. "Another lovely member of the Fenton family," he said before turning to Lord Hickington. He merely nodded and said, "Good day, Hickington. I see you've paid a call on Lady Georgiana after all."

"Yes, your grace. I felt it my duty, given that we are friends of long standing."

"Well, I bid you good day. Lady Georgiana and I have much work to do with my brother's papers."

Chapter 10

Alex had stiffened when he walked into that drawing room and saw the smug Lord Hickington sitting there paying court to Georgiana. (Since the overwhelming passion of their kiss, Alex would never again be able to think of her as *Lady* Georgiana.) At White's the night the men had met, Alex had told Hickington she wasn't seeing callers. Yet she had consented to receive the intrusive fellow—much to Alex's consternation.

Alex had, therefore, been most happy to snub the damned Hickington.

When he and Georgiana entered the library, she closed the door. "I need to speak to you about what happened last night."

He smiled. "I enjoyed kissing you very much, Georgiana."

Her face clouded. "You are *not* to call me Georgiana, and you are never to repeat such an action as you—no, as *we*—participated in last night. It's not right. Your brother has just been buried."

"I meant no disrespect to you or to the memory of my brother." He'd vow she had never kissed Freddie as she'd kissed him. Was that why she was consumed with such guilt? "I suppose you're going to make me wait for a suitable mourning period before repeating it."

She put hands to her hips. "You're not to *ever*

repeat it! It's not right."

He shook his head solemnly. "You're wrong about that, Georgiana. Nothing's ever felt so right, and you know it very well. You just don't want to acknowledge that you desire me far more than you ever desired the man to whom you were betrothed."

"That's not true!"

He moved to her, looked down into her fiery eyes, and spoke huskily. "You're lying." He went to encircle her in his arms, but she slithered away from his grasp.

"I shan't welcome you to Hartworth House any more if you're going to continue to try to seduce me."

"But think, my dear Georgiana, how dreary your life would be without me to ruffle your practiced composure."

"You're to address me as *Lady* Georgiana."

He did not respond.

"I will own," she said, almost with capitulation, "I do enjoy having someone with whom to share Freddie's papers—and to discuss unveiling his murderer."

He threw up his arms. "I am here for you to command."

She seemed to relax. "Did you go to White's last night?"

"I did. And I had the opportunity to speak to Sir Arthur."

Her brows lifted. "I do most consumingly want to know what you learned from him."

"We were right. He's completely besotted over Sophia Langston."

She gleamed.

"But I don't think he's capable of murdering

Freddie in a fit of jealousy. You see, he seemed genuinely grateful to my brother for tossing him his discarded mistress. And I think he felt honored to be among Freddie's small circle of *friends*."

She bristled. "Why did you say *friends* as you said it? Are you inferring that Freddie didn't have any friends?"

"Even Sir Arthur knew my brother well enough to know how difficult it was to be a close friend to Freddie. Surely, you realized that about him. I thought you two exchanged thousands of letters."

"Hundreds."

"I stand corrected."

"I never thought about it before. Freddie seemed only interested in being married and in starting a family. I never thought to question how odd it was that so privileged a young man did not partake of the dissolute practices other young men did—other than retaining a mistress he saw only occasionally."

He nodded. "Last night I told a falsehood—one in addition to the one that Freddie died in his sleep."

She gave him a quizzing look.

"I haven't lied since my earliest years at Eton."

"A big lie?"

"No, a very small one. To keep from showing my hand about Freddie's murder, I said I was asking the personal questions to determine who were my brother's closest friends because Freddie had a small bequest that each of his closest friends would receive a bottle of his special brandy."

"I would say that was definitely a very white lie. In fact, since it would never harm anyone in any way, I wouldn't even call it a lie."

"Ah, a pragmatic woman. What a rarity."

"And I do suppose everyone who knew Freddie also knew how much he valued his brandy."

"Exactly."

"Why do you say you don't think Sir Arthur could have killed Freddie?"

He came to sit across from her. "When I told him about the brandy, he said that even though it would be excellent brandy—likely the best he would ever own—he didn't think he'd be able to drink it. He would want to save it in memory of Freddie."

Her eyes misted. Good Lord, had she really been in love with Freddie? A woman in mourning, though, did not dress as she had today. Had she dressed so fetchingly for him? He put a gentle hand on her forearm. "Enough maudlin talk. Let's read more of the correspondence from members of the shooting party."

The long writing desk remained as it had been the previous night. He waited for her to sit, then took a seat opposite her. "You didn't read any more after I left?" he asked. Had the kiss affected her so profoundly that she'd been unable to continue going over the correspondence?

She drew a breath. "I had other things to do."

She was lying.

Before he started reading, he said, "I'm thinking of making myself known to Sophia Langston."

She set down the letter she was about to read. "For what purpose?"

He shrugged. "I want to know if she was angry when Freddie dismissed her."

Georgiana's gaze trailed over him. "As much as you resemble your brother—except you're more muscular—she could easily transfer her affections to you. Is that what you want?"

"I have no intentions of taking an actress for my mistress."

"But Freddie gave me to believe that you have a long history of dalliances with actresses."

"I refuse to discuss any past *dalliances* with you, but I do deny having ever taken any actress under my protection."

Her obsidian eyes flashed with mirth. "And I am aware that you do not tell falsehoods."

Unlike her. The obstinate woman refused to be truthful about her own feelings. And lack of feelings. "My reverence for truth is no laughing matter, Georgiana."

"Don't call me that!"

He would *not* accommodate her demand. "You cannot order me." He folded his arms across his chest. "I'm a duke."

Her eyes narrowed. "And quite an arrogant one."

He shrugged.

"So now you're going to try to charm Mrs. Langston?"

"Heavens no! I merely wish to gauge if she were angry with my brother—angry enough to want to kill him."

Georgiana leveled a stern gaze at him. "Have you forgotten the house was locked that night?"

"Have you forgotten that Mrs. Langston wasn't there?"

"It's not removed from the realm of possibility that she paid a servant to do the evil deed."

God, he hoped it wasn't their longtime coachman. The poor man might have had good reason to wish Freddie dead. "I think you should wait until we exonerate all other suspects."

He couldn't help but wonder if she wanted to keep him from seeing the actress. He eyed her with a mischievous gleam. "Could you possibly be jealous?"

She glared at him. "You're unspeakably arrogant."

He shrugged. "By the way, Sinjin—er, Lord Slade's wife has invited you to their Tuesday morning meetings."

"As did Lady Warwick, but are they not Whig gatherings?"

"The ladies *are* uncommonly interested in matters of government. The wives of my two best friends, both Lady Slade and Lady Wycliff, have been meeting long before they married men who just happen to hold the same views they do."

Her brows lowered. "Then they *are* Whigs?" She said it much as one would say, "There's a viper in my soup."

"Yes."

"You know very well the members of my family have always been Tories."

"So were mine, but I've been enlightened—as has my sister Margaret. I should have thought an independent, *intelligent* woman such as you would not be blinded by opinions of long-dead ancestors."

Her pretty head tilted to one side. "So you *do* find me intelligent?"

"For a woman." He couldn't resist revisiting the banter they'd initiated during their coach journey.

She picked up a quill from the desk and hurled it at him. Its recently sharpened tip slashed across his face.

Her eyes rounded, her face blanched. She shrieked and leapt from her chair.

He didn't not know the quill had drawn blood until he felt it trickling down his cheek.

"Oh, your grace! I'm so wretchedly sorry. I didn't mean to injure you." She whirled around the table to him and lifted her skirt to blot the blood from his face.

"Don't ruin your dress!"

She continued pressing the snowy white linen to his scratch with a gentleness that was at odds with her little fit of anger. "My maid's terribly clever about removing stains." She was not in the least self-conscious that she was presenting to him the ivory shift beneath her dress.

He averted his gaze.

"Does it hurt?"

He tossed his head back and chuckled. "I've experienced significantly worse."

She sighed. "I think the bleeding's stopped, but I fear you're going to be displaying a rather nasty gash for a while." She stood back. Their eyes met. "Are you sure it doesn't hurt?"

"I didn't say it doesn't hurt," he said with a grin. "It stings like the devil."

"I feel beastly. Can you ever forgive me?"

His gaze went to her stained dress. "You've more than earned forgiveness by sacrificing your lovely dress. And you looked so beautiful today."

Their gazes met and held. Neither spoke.

Then the door was eased open and Lady Hartworth came limping into the chamber.

Alex stood and came to her, proffering his arm. "Should your ladyship like to sit upon the sofa?"

"I would actually prefer a chair if you would be so kind as to pull up another chair where you two are sitting."

"Mama, we are dealing with the late duke's

private correspondence. I'm not comfortable sharing it with others, even you."

"But, my darling, I took the liberty of reading some of it this morning before you came down. After all, it was just sitting there in the dinner room for anyone to read."

"You are not to do that again!"

Alex dragged a chair to the table and helped her sit.

"It really was shabby the way you and the duke left me alone with Lord Hickson when it was obvious the poor man is pining away for you."

"Hickington," Georgiana said.

"I feel no guilt," Alex said. "I told the man just two nights earlier that Lady Georgiana was not receiving callers."

"He did presume a stronger attachment than ever was merited," Georgiana said. "I don't believe I'd spoken a word to him in the past two years."

"Well, there you have it," Lady Hartworth said. "I wish these tiresome young men would not call."

"I shall endeavor to spread the word that Lady Georgiana is not receiving callers."

Lady Hartworth's gaze leapt to her daughter's dress. "What's happened to your dress?" Her brows lowered. "Have you been hurt?" There was panic in her voice.

Georgiana shook her head. "No. I unintentionally injured his grace with my quill, and my dress was all I had to staunch the flow of blood."

It was then that the dowager peered at his face. "How dreadful! Does it hurt very much?" Before he could answer, she continued. "I do hope that handsome face won't be scarred."

"'Tis merely a scratch," he said.

"Mama, I am persuaded that his grace dislikes your praise as much as I dislike it when you praise me. Men are not comfortable being told they're handsome."

He turned and smiled at the dowager. "Your ladyship could never do anything that would displease me."

"Thank you, your grace." Lady Hartworth's attention returned to Georgiana. "I do believe the new Duke of Fordham is much the worthier suitor than his brother."

"The new Duke of Fordham is *not* my suitor!"

Alex turned to the older lady. "Your daughter doesn't think it proper to transfer her affections to the late duke's brother." He rather enjoyed embarrassing Georgiana.

"It wasn't as if she were actually *married* to the late duke." Lady Hartworth said. "And . . . she doesn't even have the stigma that's attached to one who breaks a betrothal. The betrothal was broken in the most honorable fashion."

Her eyes flashing with anger, Georgiana's gaze flicked from her mother to him. "Both of you are incorrigible!"

"But, darling, you're not even marrying warning for the poor, dead duke."

"Wearing mourning," Georgiana corrected.

Lady Hartworth once again mock slapped her own face. "I said marrying warning, did I not?"

"You did," Georgiana said.

"I know exactly what I meant to say. It just doesn't come out the right way."

"It's all right, Mama," Georgiana said in a tender voice. "We knew what you meant. It may take some time before you're back to where you were before your affliction."

Georgiana's disagreements with her mother in no way reflected the inherent tenderness in their close relationship. This was a side to her he admired vastly.

A pity she was so heartless in her associations with men: with Freddie, with him, even with Lord Hickington.

"I hate that you've gone and ruined your appearance," Lady Hartworth said to her daughter. "I beg that you run along and put on another dress. One without blood. And I do hope Angelique can get that stain out. You're so lovely in that dress."

"If your maid is unsuccessful with the blood stains," he said, "I would be honored if you'd allow me to order you another dress." He rather fancied selecting exactly what he'd like to see her wear, though it would be difficult to look prettier than she had looked today. Of course, she would never let him.

"I am sure that won't be necessary." Georgiana left the chamber.

He turned to the mother. "Alas, I must take my leave, but I beg that you allow me to walk you to where you're going."

She rose and settled a hand upon his proffered arm.

$\mathcal{C}$hapter 11

Sinjin and Wycliff were just driving up to his house in Berkley Square when Alex arrived home. They disembarked from Wycliff's coach as Alex dismounted.

"We've come to collect you," Wycliff said.

Alex's gaze whisked over the two. They were dressed far more formally than he. "What for?" He handed off his horse to a footman, who walked it around to the mews.

"Since you're now officially in the House of Lords, we wanted to accompany you to your first session this first afternoon."

Sinjin smiled. "After all these years, the three of us will be as one again, just like at Eton."

Alex smiled to himself. If one of them got into a schoolboy fight, the opponent had been shunned by the other two. If one joined the chess club, the other two followed. *We three will be as one*, they often said. And nothing in the ensuing years ever diminished the allegiance they held for one another.

"It's rather important that you join us because the discussion of increasing the money for Wellington's army will be taken up," Wycliff added.

A proposal Freddie had been wholly against. Alex knew how vital it was that the British defeat Napoleon. No matter how much money it cost to beef up the armies and the Royal Navy, it was money well spent. Otherwise, their country would end up under French domination. And all Englishmen would be speaking French.

The men began to mount the steps to the front door of Fordham House. He still could not believe he was master of the finest house on Berkley Square. From beneath the fanlight window, the wide shiny black door eased open, courtesy of another footman, and the three of them entered. An elegant stairway curved down to the checkerboard marble floor they crossed to reach the library. "I'm not sure I ought to go with you," Alex said.

"Why not?" Sinjin asked.

"Because I've only just inherited. Would it not be unseemly if I gleefully took my brother's place in the House of Lords less than two weeks after his death—promulgating everything he opposed?"

Sinjin harrumphed. "It's not as if your brother ever took his seat. Except for giving lip service to the damned Tories, he was almost apolitical."

"Even though that's true, I shouldn't like to give the impression I'm racing along with political ambitions so soon after Freddie's tragic death."

"Those who know you and your recently hard-fought campaign for the House of Commons would think it unseemly if you suddenly lost interest in those matters over which you were so passionate just weeks ago," Wycliff said.

"There is that," Alex said with a shrug.

"And were you not prepared to deliver your maiden address in the House of Commons on just this matter we're to discuss tonight?" Sinjin asked.

"I was to have delivered it last Monday," Alex said solemnly.

Wycliff's dark eyes met his. "Then do so tonight."

Alex stood at the cabinet and poured three glasses of Madeira and handed two of them off. "You're sure I won't be considered insensitive?"

"Wear full mourning attire," Wycliff suggested.

Dressed entirely in black, Margaret came into the room. "I thought I heard voices," she said, her gaze scanning the group. Alex's friends came forward and bowed and kissed and gave the proper greetings. Alex urged her to sit with them.

She sat on the sofa near the fire.

"We hope we've just persuaded your brother to take his seat in the House of Lords this afternoon," Sinjin said.

Her face brightened. "Then will you deliver what was to have been your maiden address in the House of Commons? It was such a fine speech." Margaret, who had become fast friends with Wycliff's and Sinjin's reforming wives, had been kind enough to listen to him rehearsing and had added a few salient points to his talk.

"You don't think it would make me look uncaring? About Freddie's death?" Especially since Freddie had made no bones about his objection to raising more money for the military. When all was said and done, Freddie was mostly interested in Freddie. And Freddie disliked any measure that would make him have to pay a farthing more in taxes. Alex had been proud of Margaret for standing up against Freddie for Alex and his politics.

She thought for a moment before answering. "I think those who've kept up with your short-but-very-fruitful Parliamentary career would be offended if you suddenly dropped your championship of the military funding bill. But . . . you must wear full mourning."

As awkward as it would be to take Freddie's place so soon after his death, Alex knew it would be wrong to turn his back on all the work he'd done since being elected to Parliament. "Very well."

* * *

Georgiana was stunned when she read the morning newspapers. The *Morning Chronicle* printed the full text of a speech Fordham had delivered the previous night in the House of Lords. He had—she reluctantly admitted—eloquently spoken in favor of the military funding to which Freddie had so violently objected. Her brother also opposed the measure. How dare Fordham disrespect his departed brother in such a manner!

As angry as she was, she read on.

The newly succeeded Duke of Fordham's highly regarded speech was met with raucous cheering— even by several noted Tories who were stirred by Fordham's patriotism when he said, "England cannot afford NOT to put every effort it can into winning this war. As Lord Nelson so poignantly put it on the very night before he gave his life for England, England expects that every man will do his duty.'"

The Duke of Fordham is carrying on with the stellar leadership he demonstrated in his short career in the House of Commons where he was the Member for Blythstone. Whig grandees appear to be grooming this ex-soldier to be First Lord of the Treasury.

First Lord of the Treasury? This man who'd disrespected his brother's memory was in line to lead the nation? He might even have murdered his brother. He *was* the one who would benefit the most from Freddie's death.

In the short time she had come to know him, though, she did not believe him capable of murdering his brother. His reverence of truth, his deep, lifelong friendship with the highly respected Lord Slade, the allegiance of his sisters, all pointed to Fordham's innocence. Yet she kept remembering that his own mother had feared he might kill Freddie. Or vice versa.

Later that day, his sister, Lady Margaret, called at Hartworth House. She came with Lady Slade and Lady Wycliff. Georgiana had been mesmerized by the uncommon blonde beauty of Lord Wycliff's wife. Her face was perfection, a perfect porcelain oval with large blue eyes, full lips and even white teeth, all framed with hair the colour of wheat shimmering in the noonday sun. Her morning dress and matching pelisse were of pale blue, the exact shade of her eyes and flawlessly constructed in impeccable taste.

Then Georgiana's attention turned to Lady Slade. It was difficult to tell what that lady's age was for she looked so very youthful with a smattering of freckles across her pert nose. Her Christian name was Jane, and no lady could be more of a plain Jane as far as appearances went. Her hair was an unmemorable shade of brown, and her green eyes were unremarkable. At first Georgiana was surprised that a handsome peer such as Lord Slade, who was perhaps too large for Georgiana's taste, had fallen in love with the lady. Was she an heiress? Then Georgiana remembered Lord Slade had married a Featherstone. Everyone knew the respectable Featherstones, though having aristocratic connections, did not have a feather to fly with.

But the more Georgiana observed Lady Slade, the more she realized there was something special, an indefinable spark about her countenance.

"I've been dying to make you known to my dear friends," Lady Margaret said to Georgiana after the introductions. "I have been friends with Lady Slade for many years, and for many of those years Lady Wycliff, before she was Lady Wycliff, was hostess to the most wondrous Tuesday gatherings." She sighed. "I have Lady Slade to thank for introducing me to those gatherings, and it's my fondest hope now that you're in London you'll be joining us."

"I am flattered by your attentions," Georgiana said. "But do those gatherings not appeal to Whig philosophy?"

"Don't worry about that," Lady Margaret assured. "My family—except for dear Alex, er, Fordham—has always followed or led the Tories, but I pride myself on my ability to make my own decisions based upon my informed mind." She came and clasped Georgiana's hand. "And now that you're at liberty to be in London with your mama, I know you'll see the light."

Georgiana had led the group to the drawing room where they sat almost in a semi-circle. "I confess to being ill informed on political philosophy."

"I do hope you read about Fordham's speech in the *Morning Chronicle*," Lady Margaret said.

"I did."

"What did you think?" Lady Margaret was incapable of *not* looking inordinately pleased.

Georgiana did not know how to respond. Obviously Lady Margaret did not think the present duke had done anything wrong. And Georgiana had, after all, been friends with Lady Margaret these past several years. She did not want to offend her. "It appears that his grace gave a most inspiring, well-accepted speech. His maiden one, I believe?"

Lady Margaret's smile stretched from ear to ear. "It was wonderful. He practiced it with me—before he had to go north."

"Does it not bother you that the new duke is promulgating something to which his predecessor objected?" Georgiana asked. Lady Margaret was, after all, sister to the late duke as well.

"Sweet saints, no! Freddie, as dearly as I loved him, was the perfect example of a closed-minded peer who only sought his own interests." Margaret shrugged. "Freddie was the kind of man who would have worn a white wig long after the practice died simply because he didn't like change."

That was true. The same could be said for Georgiana's brother. "But do you not feel guilty for turning your back on the things your family has always stood for?"

Lady Margaret squinted at her. "My grandfather had plantations in the West Indies. He owned slaves. I will never condone that. Could you, my dear Lady Georgiana?"

"No, I don't suppose I could."

"We will never try to bludgeon you with our ideas," Lady Slade said, "but we'd be so gratified if you'd come just once. It's not as if we're asking you to attend the Wycliffs' political dinners where everyone is a Member of Parliament or the spouse of one."

The beautiful Lady Wycliff smiled. "Lady Margaret says that you're intelligent, and I believe you'll be happy to surround yourself with a room full of other ladies of similar intellectual capabilities."

Now that intrigued Georgiana. She did want to demonstrate to that obstinate Fordham that she wasn't just intelligent *for a woman*! "Then I shall come on Tuesday." She turned to Lady Slade. "I understand you are recently wed."The bride's face went from ordinary to celestial in the span of second. Her eyes seemed brighter, her smile ethereal, her lowered lashes longer. "Yes. I have the rare privilege of enjoying heaven in my third decade on earth."

Lady Wycliff giggled. "You see," she said to Georgiana, "Jane had adored Sinjin since she was fourteen years of age."

"Sinjin - - -" Lady Margaret started.

"Is Lord Slade," Georgiana said, nodding. "Yes, I deduced that during the many hours I shared a coach with him and the new Duke of Fordham."

"And no two people could be of more similar temperament and interests than Sinjin and Jane. It's a perfect marriage." Lady Margaret turned to Lady Wycliff. "As is your match with Lord Wycliff."

Georgiana sighed and looked at Lady Margaret. "I do hope you find a mate as compatible. And me, too, now. . ."

Their eyes all lowered. Freddie was gone. Her betrothal had been severed by death. She was once again a spinster. It was doubtful she would ever marry.

Now—now that she had kissed the scandalous Fordham—she had a new impediment to finding a compatible mate. In the past, she'd rejected suitors who were dull or dim-witted or ugly or profligate. Now she would never be able to plight her life to one whose kisses did not move her as Fordham's had. Even the memory of being held in his arms caused her heart to race.

She must change the subject. Turning her attention to Lady Margaret, she said, "I suppose your sisters are grateful they need only mourn three months, so they'll be able to participate later in the Season."

"Three months is a respectable period," Lady Margaret said with a nod. "When one is but seventeen, a year or six months is such a large percentage of one's life. A mourning of such length would be crushing."

An intelligent observation, to be sure, Georgiana thought. Perhaps she would enjoy belonging to the group of Tuesday ladies.

Georgiana looked down at her own rose-coloured dress. "As much as I wish to honor the late duke, I've always abhorred it when those unrelated to the deceased mourn for him. You see it so much when one of the Royal Family dies and so many pretentious people adopt mourning garb as if to create a connection to the loftier personage."

Lady Margaret nodded. "Mourning should be a personal decision. Though I think of you as family, my dear Lady Georgiana, I appreciate that you're cognizant you're still a Fenton."

"One who makes her own decisions and is not bound by what others expect is just the type of person our group welcomes," Lady Wycliff said. "You, Lady Georgiana, are possessed of the ability to be a free thinker. I just wish more members of

Parliament were."

Georgiana had never thought of herself as a free thinker. Her family had always been Tories. She had never before questioned their political affiliations. Still, she could not imagine embracing the Whigs. She'd been brought up to rank them only slightly above those in lunatic asylums. On the other hand, she was flattered that these obviously intelligent ladies thought her capable of independent thinking. Poor, dear Freddie certainly was *not*. "Thank you, Lady Wycliff."

"How are you coming with Freddie's papers?" Lady Margaret asked.

"Sorting them has been a formidable task. I confess I feel like a voyeur even thinking about reading them, but I am most curious to read those from a certain actress."

Lady Margaret's brows plummeted. "Then you knew about her?"

Georgiana nodded. "Am I being gullible in believing he broke it off after I accepted his offer?"

"Not at all. It's the truth." Lady Margaret turn to the two married ladies. "My late brother appointed Lady Georgiana as custodian of all his papers."

Lady Slade's eyes widened. "That sounds a daunting task."

"It's just the type of activity I like," Georgiana said.

"No one could do a better job. Of that I'm sure." Lady Margaret stood. "We must be off, but before we go I'd like to say hello to your mother."

Georgiana got up and began walking toward the morning room that was now her mother's bedchamber. "She'll be delighted. Just don't mention the Whigs," Georgiana said. "Papa was violently opposed to them, and Mama was and still is his puppet though he's been gone a half dozen years."

* * *

This was the first day since Freddie's death that Alex hadn't seen Georgiana. The closeness that had developed between them in so short a period perplexed him. He knew he could cut it off at any time, but strangely he didn't want to. He looked forward to seeing her every day. He thought she, too, enjoyed being with him, although she would be loath to acknowledge it.

As much as he wanted to be with her, he fought it. This one day he would prove that he could stay away. She'd been right. He should not covet his dead brother's betrothed. It was disrespectful of Freddie.

Perhaps he would make himself known to Mrs. Langston today. He smiled to himself as he remembered Georgiana's opposition to his meeting with the actress. Could she be jealous? When Mannings announced his cousin, Alex decided Sophia Langston could be put off another day.

He went from his library to meet Robert in the broad entry corridor. He was happy to see him. Robert Cecil, though a first cousin, bore little resemblance to the Havershams. He had most decidedly taken after his Scottish mother with his red hair, ruddy complexion, and clear blue eyes. He had even inherited the Gordons' propensity toward spreading girth. As to his temperament, he was far jollier than Alex or his brothers had ever been. That was why he'd always been such a great favorite with the Haversham brothers.

As was fitting to the graveness of the occasion, Robert's face was solemn. "I had to come straight away after I heard the shattering news of Freddie's death. I'm so very sorry."

Alex put an arm around him. "So good of you to come. I've been wanting to speak to those of you who were with him his last day on earth. Let's go to the library."

Alex poured brandy, and the two sat in front of the library's fire. He felt wretchedly guilty that he was forced to hide the truth about Freddie's murder from their own cousin, but as Georgiana had urged, he must consider every member of that final shooting party as a suspect. Even though he knew Robert Cecil incapable of committing murder.

Robert sipped his brandy, shaking his head. "I still can't believe he's gone. Such a young man in the prime of life—and in such apparently good health." He turned to Alex. "It's some consolation to remember that he was in good spirits that day. I hadn't seen him so happy since . . . well, to be honest, I'd never seen him happier."

"It *is* consolation to know his last day was a happy one."

"He was gleeful that he and Lady Georgiana were to marry in just a few weeks. He was totally besotted over her. And he was also happy because he'd had an excellent day shooting. Made the rest of us look like novices."

"And the group was congenial? No spoilsports?"

"I thought it was surprisingly congenial. You know Freddie had not your flair for making friends, especially close friendships like with you and Wycliff and Slade, nor did he have your talent for endearing himself to others—and to women as you do—but he had gathered about him all of us who got along remarkably well with him." Robert looked up from the rim of his glass to meet Alex's gaze. "I feel beastly guilty that I never cared for him as much as I cared for you."

Alex felt even more guilty for not being completely honest with Robert. "Don't feel guilty. Even though he was my brother, I always preferred *you* over him."

Robert's brows lowered. "Why were you asking about spoilsports?"

"I just wondered if there had been any unpleasantness that could have provoked a fatal attack. It's so perplexing that a healthy young man just expired in his sleep."

"It's as if our family is cursed. First Richard. Now Freddie."

It was so difficult for Alex to bring up the possible motive for Robert to kill Freddie, Alex didn't broach the subject for a moment. "Yes, it's most distressing, old fellow. And if something happens to me, you're next in line."

"God forbid! That never crossed my mind—not when there were three strapping sons to carry on when Uncle died." His eyes misted. "It's bad enough losing Freddie. Losing you would be more than a body could bear."

Such powerful emotions could not be feigned.

Another suspect exonerated.

$\mathcal{C}$hapter 12

"I'm not going with you to visit an actress." Wycliff folded his arms across his chest. "I have Louisa to consider."

Alex had been in the process of handing his hat off to Harry Wycliff's butler when he snapped it back. "But Sophia Langston might be culpable in . . . a certain . . . sibling's death."

"Why can you not go alone?"

"Lady Georgiana thinks that might send the message that I'm interested in securing Mrs. Langston's affections." He felt like a lad hiding behind a woman's skirts, but he could hardly say that the actress *could* want to transfer her affections to him because of his strong resemblance to Freddie and because he *was* a duke. That would make him sound conceited.

Wycliff eyed him quizzically, a smirk on his face. "She does, does she? You know what I think?"

"As close as we are, Harry, I am not privy to your thoughts."

"I think Lady Georgiana Fenton has developed a *tendré* for you. She's jealous of Sophia Langston. I also believe—and Sinjin agrees with me upon this—you and Lady Georgiana are well suited for each other."

Alex rolled his eyes. "We're consoling one another. We each lost a loved one. Reading anything more into it could tarnish the lady's reputation."

"It would take much more than that to tarnish her upstanding reputation. She's the unblemished daughter of a marquess. Louisa assures me she's intelligent, too, and Louisa's an excellent judge of character. Lady Georgiana Fenton would never ruin herself by making unsound decisions."

Alex could not purge his mind of the ferocity of Georgiana's passion. Would she ever allow herself to give in to it? God, but he wished he could be the fortunate recipient.

He started to walk away. "Then I'll see if I can persuade Sinjin to accompany me."

"We'll meet this evening at the Palace of Westminster?"

"I'll be there." The military funding bill was very important to him.

* * *

As it happened, Sinjin was not at home, nor was his wife. Alex would have to go alone to see the actress. He knew from Freddie's papers that his brother had set up Mrs. Langston in an older house in St. James. Though he always preferred to ride his horse—and a wonderful specimen of horseflesh Fleetania was—he decided to arrive at Mrs. Langston's place in the ducal-crested coach. He only hoped the poor woman wasn't seized with apoplexy when a man who so resembled her former lover arrived in the former lover's coach.

Sophia Langston's house clad in the red bricks so prominent a century earlier was much more impressive than what he'd expected. Its Palladian embellishments of fan-shaped windows and white pediments over the doorways and windows gave it a sophisticated air. He was relieved there were no other gentlemen's coaches in front.

As befitted his rank, his coachman knocked upon the lady's door, and when it was answered, he presented Alex's newly printed card. Alex hoped to God she didn't mistake him for Freddie.

A moment later, the butler returned and nodded to the coachman, signaling that Alex would be welcomed by the woman who had long been the toast of the London stage.

Alex was shown to the upstairs drawing room. It was furnished expensively in gilded French chairs and silken sofas of turquoise. Draperies of the same hue had been lifted away from the windows to allow sunlight into the chamber.

Mrs. Langston kept him waiting for half an hour. When she finally strolled into the chamber, his first thought was, *She looks older in person than she looks on stage.* He'd seen her several weeks earlier in a popular satire that was so well received, it was hard at times to hear the actors because of the audience's roars of laughter.

Today she dressed tastefully in a dove gray, very fine muslin dress trimmed in white lace. Even her white gloves were ornamented with sprigs of lace. The litheness of her figure disguised her advancing years. Her brown hair was shorn in a youthful style but there was nothing youthful about the deep indentations on either side of her mouth or the sagging flesh beneath her chin. He'd thought she must be in her mid-thirties. Now he knew he'd missed the mark by a decade.

Her mouth gaped open when she beheld him. Her eyes misted. "You're almost the image of the late duke!"

He nodded as he stepped forward to bow and kiss her hand. "We've been told that most of our lives."

She ran an eye down the length of his torso. "You're more muscular."

"He was an indolent nobleman, I a soldier."

"And now you're to be the indolent nobleman! It is a very great honor to meet you, your grace. Won't you please sit and visit with me?"

His sweeping arm gesture indicated for her to sit first. She sat in the center of the sofa. He chose a chair facing her.

"I shall never forget the first time I saw you on the stage," he began. "No one has ever played Ophelia with such perfection." He started to tell her how beautiful he'd thought her but, remembering Georgiana's words, he feared he'd be sending the wrong message. The last thing he wanted was for her to think he wished to be her protector.

He clearly understood why Freddie had dismissed this woman after falling in love with Georgiana.

She smiled. "*Hamlet*. I did love that role—and the play. You must have been a mere lad."

He chuckled. "I was. Eighteen. Just before I went to Spain."

"I'm honored you still remember it." Her voice was easily recognizable, yet different from the projection of her stage voice. There was a velvety timbre to her conversational voice.

They sat there facing each other for a moment, neither willing to start. Finally, she said, "My deepest sympathies on the death of your brother. I will confess this is the first time I've been able to speak of it without launching into tears. The first night after I heard the heartbreaking news, I could not perform. I could not staunch the flow of my tears." She shrugged her dainty shoulders. "It's silly, I know. We had parted more than a year earlier, and there's a new man in my life who's exceedingly devoted, yet still my heart broke for your brother."

There was no malice in her words or tone when she spoke of Freddie. "I'm gratified you speak of him with affection."

She bestowed a bright smile on Alex. "So . . . to what do I owe the pleasure of your visit, your grace?"

His lips clamped together. "It's difficult to explain. If you knew my brother well—and I'm not sure anyone really did—you'd know we weren't close. I'm trying to learn about him during the last . . ." He almost said *days* but remembered Freddie hadn't seen her in a year. ". . .year of his life. As his successor, I feel compelled to carry on as he would have." Which was partially true. Except in Parliament.

She gave a bitter laugh. "You are right. Your brother was like some distant God to me. I worshipped him but never knew him. The year I spent under his protection was the happiest and the most miserable year of my life." Her soft green eyes lifted. "Does that sound too ridiculously stupid?"

"Not at all. I think I understand."

"You see, when he was with me—which wasn't often—I was deliriously happy. When he was away, I felt great melancholy. I knew that a duke as young and handsome as he could easily win the affections of the most perfect being—which I know I am not. I tortured myself worrying that I would lose his affections." She gave a little feminine chuckle. "And, of course, eventually I did."

The most perfect being. Georgiana. He swallowed hard. "A man does not leave so generous a settlement to a woman he doesn't care for. I believe my brother's separation from you was motivated by honor. He was merely honorable enough to want to be a true and faithful husband to the woman he was going to marry." Hopefully, this rationalization would assuage some of her sense of rejection.

"You're very kind, your grace. I'm embarrassed that you know of my settlement, but I suppose it's only natural that all of the late duke's papers have fallen to you."

Rather than allow this woman to know that Lady Georgiana Fenton could already have read Mrs. Langston's personal letters to Freddie, Alex merely nodded.

"Then I should like to ask you a favor," she said.

His eyebrows lifted.

"Could I persuade you to return my letters?"

He had not expected this and was unprepared to answer. While he did not want to lie, he did not want to reveal the truth, either. "Are you sure my brother kept them?"

Her shoulders shrugged. "I thought you would know."

"I've mostly been concerning myself with his legal papers." Which was *mostly* true.

She nodded. "I'm afraid I'm not particularly helpful about enlightening you about your brother since he succeeded, but I think you were right when you said it wasn't likely anyone really knew him."

"You speak of my brother with such affection.

Did he never ignite anger in you? I know as lads, he and I fought each other like savages," he said, grinning.

She tossed back her head and laughed. "I don't remember ever being angry with him, but that is more a testament to my placid nature. He *was* most negligent of me."

"Negligent?"

"Because he so seldom came to the Capital. In other ways, he was exceedingly generous. You will probably learn just how generous if you come across the bills of sale from Rundell and Bridge jewelers. I could live comfortably the rest of my life off the proceeds of the jewelry he gave me." She drew a deep breath, and when she spoke, her voice cracked. "If I could ever part with anything I received from him."

Alex no longer even thought about her aging, or how different she looked in person, or how poorly she compared with Georgiana. As he sat there speaking with her, he thought she was a lovely, gracious woman who'd been deeply in love with Freddie. She could no more have killed Freddie than he could have.

Another suspect exonerated.

* * *

Even though she was enthralled with Freddie's papers, Georgiana needed to get away from Hartworth House if only for a little while. So she actually looked forward to joining Lady Margaret at the Tuesday gathering at Wycliff House.

Lady Margaret had collected her in the Fordham ducal coach. "My brother prefers his horse. In fact, he loves that horse as much as he loves his sisters! He hasn't yet taken to the formalities of being a duke. He goes about acting as if he were still a soldier just returned from the Peninsula."

Indeed, Georgiana had thought the very same thing about him. She could not recall any duke ever traversing about the Capital on horseback. But, then, nothing about Fordham would convey his elite status. He *did* bring to mind a rugged soldier far more than an idle nobleman.

As they neared the house on Grosvenor Square, Lady Margaret relayed an interesting story about Wycliff House. "Lord Wycliff's father gambled away the house, and when Lord Wycliff was able to restore the family fortune, one of the first things he wanted to buy back was the Grosvenor Square House. That's how he met his wife. She had lived there with her first husband, who'd died."

"But she looks so young to have been married twice!"

"Yes. Her sister, who's also a member of the Tuesday group, told us that Lady Wycliff —the former Mrs. Phillips—was forced into marriage with an older man when she was only fifteen. Lady Wycliff refuses to talk of it. I believe she's four and twenty now."

"The same as me," Georgiana said in a whisper.

At the Grosvenor Square house, Lady Wycliff greeted Georgiana and showed her to the drawing room where a dozen young women had gathered in gilt chairs arranged in a circle. Lady Slade, looking very sweet in a lavender gown, popped up from her chair and came to greet Georgiana cheerily. "Each week one of us explores a different topic," she explained. "Let me introduce you to this week's speaker, Lady Wycliff's sister, Ellie Coke."

Mrs. Coke was much younger—probably by a

half a dozen years—than the sister she so resembled. Even though the two bore a strong resemblance, the younger sister was merely pretty. Lady Wycliff was a stunning beauty.

"Mrs. Coke's husband," Lady Slade explained, "will be standing for the election to the Parliamentary seat vacated by the Duke of Fordham when he moved to the House of Lords. Mr. Coke is also Lord Wycliff's cousin."

"And I suppose your husband will stand as a Whig?" Georgiana said to Ellie Coke.

Mrs. Coke's pale blue eyes flashed with mirth. "But of course."

It was then that Georgiana recalled last year's elections when the present Duke of Fordham had successfully stood for the House of Commons for Blythstone, and Mr. Coke had been defeated in his challenge to the Tory member from Alesbury. Now that she thought of it, she recalled Fordham saying he wished to sponsor Mr. Coke for his old seat. With the duke's support—and his purse—Mr. Coke would be sure to finally take a seat in the House of Commons.

Soon all the introductions were completed, and the ladies took their seats, save Mrs. Coke, who stood to make her presentation on the concept of education for all. After her introductory remarks, she rather shocked Georgiana when she said, "The purpose of teaching the illiterate to read should *not* be to enable them to read Scripture— though we do believe being able to read Scripture a worthy skill. We believe the ignorant masses need to be exposed to *every* manner of the written word, and they will also need to be able to learn arithmetic, a useful skill for the rest of their lives."

It wasn't that Georgiana disagreed with

anything Mrs. Coke said, but to rail against the reading of God's Word was unprecedented. Georgiana's thoughts then moved to the school for girls her mother sponsored in the village of Alsop. It had been established to teach the daughters of their cottagers to read the Bible. Lady Hartworth had also encouraged the school mistress to teach the girls elementary needlework.

But what of the lads? Georgiana could not recall any school for the boys of Alsop's illiterate. How sad that young boys of the middle and upper classes received the opportunity to learn not only to read but also to learn of all the classical thinkers. But because of their station in life, sons of those who toiled were denied the same privilege.

As interesting as Mrs. Coke's presentation was, Georgiana found herself trying to imagine the deprivation of not being able to read, not being able to write a letter, not being able to learn through books of the world and its history and its people.

"To move to a more perfect society," Mrs. Coke said, "it is imperative that *all* the nation's people also be an informed electorate." Mrs. Coke smiled as her gaze moved to her sister. "But, of course, Lady Wycliff will address the expansion of the franchise next week. In conclusion, I will add that when literacy goes up, crime goes down. A well-educated man has no need to gain through misdeeds.

"But to establish schools for all boys and all girls in every corner of the kingdom will be exceedingly costly. Quite understandably, the wealthy land-owning Tories are violently opposed to diminishing their own wealth for the Greater Good."

As Mrs. Coke sat down, all the ladies applauded. It was then that Georgiana realized she was not clapping. She was stunned over the single political reference from the speaker. *Tories are violently opposed to diminishing their own wealth for the Greater Good.*

Georgiana had read enough to know the Greater Good was promulgated by Jeremy Bentham. Good Lord, were these women Benthamites? Papa—were he alive—would have apoplexy! Her brother, too.

In her four and twenty years, Georgiana had never heard anyone utter a negative word against the Tories, who had ruled England for most of her life. Mrs. Coke was attempting to tear down the wall dividing Tories and Whigs. *For the Greater Good.*

Slowly, Georgiana began to clap.

Afterward, Georgiana went to compliment her. "Thank you, Mrs. Coke, for your enlightening talk. I agree with everything you said—except your bashing of the Tories. They're not a bad lot. All my family are Tories."

Ellie Coke's features fell. "Oh, I am heartily sorry if I offended you or your family."

Her sister came and put an arm around Mrs. Coke's shoulders while addressing Georgiana. "Most of us, except for Jane Featherstone—er, I mean Jane Slade—were raised by Tories. However, we've come to believe things for the Greater Good should not be labeled either Tory or Whig. They're for Humanity."

Nodding, Georgiana relished being associated with intelligent women. "I feel honored to have attended today."

"Will you return next week?" Lady Wycliff asked

Georgiana. "I'll be speaking."

"Yes, but don't expect me to ever oppose the Tories."

"You don't have to," Lady Wycliff said. "We feel the causes we advocate are apolitical. We advocate for anything that improves the lives of everyone in Britain."

"A worthy undertaking, to be sure," Georgiana said. And she meant it.

All the way home her thoughts were on the words uttered by Lady Wycliff. She must be heavily influenced by the essayist Philip Lewis. Georgiana would be hard pressed to actually say Mr. Lewis was a Whig. His causes benefited . . . Humanity.

Georgiana could see that she would enjoy spending her Tuesdays with these brilliant women.

But of course, she could never embrace Whigs.

$\mathcal{C}$hapter 13

Georgiana would want to know about his meeting with Mrs. Langston. That's what Alex told himself as he rode Fleetania beneath gray skies from his home on Berkley Square to hers on Cavendish Square.

If he stayed away from Georgiana, would she dare come to him at Fordham House? She just might—not to see him, of course, but to satisfy her rampant curiosity about Freddie's death. She was even more interested in helping him discover the murderer than she was in reading Mrs. Langston's letters—and he had no doubts about how eager she was to indulge herself over torrid declarations from Freddie's inamorata.

Whether she knew it or not, Georgiana was possessed of simmering passions—passions he would delight in freeing. He needed to suppress the memory of their crushing kiss, of feeling her slender body pressed against his, or he'd go mad with want of her.

Seeing her was the real reason he was going to Hartworth House this afternoon.

As he entered Cavendish Square he observed Hickington, also on a mount, entering the square from the Harley Street entrance. Even from across the square, Alex was more interested in Hickington's horse than in its obstinate rider. How could a man as annoying as Hickington have so excellent an eye for horseflesh? This chestnut with white stockings was a beauty! Sixteen hands if she were an inch. And what a head! Sheer perfection.

"We meet once again at Lady Georgiana's," Hickington said when their horses drew up in front of Hartworth House. He could not have sounded more bitter were he challenging Alex to a duel.

Alex gave a curt nod, his attention drawn to the magnificent beast. He nearly complimented Hickington on his fine horse, but Alex had no desire to add to the man's perceived consequence.

Without thinking of what he was doing, Alex extended his hand in an unsuccessful attempt to smooth out a swirling patch of hair on the beast's withers. It was rather like trying to flatten grass with one's hand—an impossible task.

The Hartworth porter swung open the glossy black door which was flanked by two shiny brass lanterns. "Should you grace wish Lady Georgiana to be told you're calling?"

Alex glared at Hickington for a second before answering in the affirmative. The two men were shown to the drawing room. It was then that Alex noticed how hideously flamboyant the other man dressed. Was he actually wearing an *orange* cravat? Why would a man blessed with such height and a full head of black hair—a man who must be deemed of above-average appearance— gimmick up himself in such a manner? "I'm afraid you've once again come at a deuced bad time, old fellow," Alex said to Lord Hickington.

Hickington's eyes narrowed. "Now see here, Fordham, you can't keep the lady from seeing an old friend."

"But the lady is promised to me."

The viscount's brow rose, and the look he gave Alex said he would like to drive a fist into his face. He spoke with malice. "Is it not rather early for her to transfer her affections to the brother of her betrothed?"

"You mistake me. And you mistake Lady Georgiana if you think her so devoid of propriety. Can you truly be her friend?"

"Of course I'm her friend! What, pray tell, did you mean by her being *promised* to you?"

From the corner of his eye, Alex saw Georgiana gracefully halt at the chamber's doorway as she watched them. "I mean that Lady Georgiana and I had planned to discuss matters pertaining to my brother's will today."

Her eyes met Alex's and sparkled as she strolled into the chamber. "That's right, Lord Hickington. I'm not yet seeing callers. The duke is here in his connection with the last wishes of his late brother, my fiancé."

"But did I not see you with Lady Margaret in the Fordham coach going to Grosvenor Square yesterday?"

Was the damn man following her?

"Lady Margaret, lest you forget, is part of the late duke's family," she said. "For now, those are the only people I'm comfortable with."

"The lady wishes to be with those who share her grief," Alex said, his brows lowering as he eyed the unwelcome intruder.

Hickington turned his attention to Georgiana, and he effected a smile. "I thought, since you're not wearing mourning, that perhaps—"

"I shouldn't have to explain to you why I don't think it proper for me to wear mourning, but I assure you the decision has nothing to do with an absence of grief."

"Then my concern for you is well founded. As I told you when I last called, I feel that you need a man to look out for you since your brother remains at Alsop."

Georgiana had not taken a seat. She stood glaring down at her caller. "You are either misinformed or bereft of common sense if you believe I need a man. I am four and twenty years of age, of reasonable intelligence, and perfectly capable of looking out for myself."

Her persistent suitor cowered. "You are as intelligent as you are beautiful, my lady. Forgive me if my concern for your welfare annoys you."

Alex, who also had not taken a seat, came to stand beside Georgiana and looked down at Hickington. "Forgive us, old fellow, but we must repair to the library to look at some of my brother's papers. You'll excuse us?"

His azure eyes icy, Hickington stood. "Yes, of course."

Georgiana held out her hand for her caller to kiss. "It's very kind of you to be so solicitous of my wellbeing, my lord."

"I beg that you call for me if ever you are in need," Hickington said.

Why did the man have to hold her hand for so long, Alex wondered—not without rancor.

Once he left, Alex escorted her to the library. It was difficult for him to reconcile the ill-dressed marquess's daughter he'd met that day at Alsop to the beautifully dressed noblewoman she was today.

She wore a sea foam gown of cambric. Its waist fell just beneath her modest bosom that was covered in a contrasting white embroidered crepe from the waist to her neck, where it terminated in French lace the same shade of white. The effect was perfection.

Their entry into the library met with sheets of rain planing off the windows. "Oh, dear, poor Lord Hickington. Did he come on horseback?"

Alex nodded. "A very fine horse it was."

"It was wicked of you to tell Lord Hickington I was promised to you," she chided.

He playfully raised a brow. "So you heard that."

"I did, indeed." She sighed. "Though I will own, I was grateful to you for ridding me of that man's presence."

Alex stopped in his stride and looked down at her. "I was merely eliminating my competition. Wouldn't any woman be honored to be courted by a well-looking man of fashion like Lord Hickington? I must ask where he procured his cravat."

She swatted his arm. "It was hideous, and you know it."

He gazed at his arm. "There you go, trying to injure me again."

She turned to observe his face and spoke gently. "Your wound looks better today. I still feel beastly about it."

Thump. Thump. Lady Hartworth came down the hall. "You haven't injured his highness again, have you, Georgiana?"

"Grace, not highness," the daughter corrected, turning to face her mother. "After the scolding you gave me following my last mindless assault, I hope I'm sure to never again injure his grace." Under her breath, she added, "Even though he provokes me."

Alex bowed at the dowager and mocked kissed her hand. "You look lovely today, Lady Hartworth."

"Such a gallant you are, your grace." Her ladyship preened while availing herself of the duke's proffered arm. "Are you two going to be cloistering yourselves in the library again?"

"Indeed we are," Alex said.

Lady Hartworth compressed her lips as she stood at the room's entrance. "I am not allowed in there."

"Why not?" he asked.

"My daughter forbids it. She says she doesn't trust me not to be reading the late duke's personal papers, that they're . . . well, personal. I do find it appallingly bad taste to entrust an innocent maiden like Georgiana with reading love letters from one's mistress."

Georgiana rolled her eyes. "Mama was caught reading letters from an actress who shall remain unnamed."

"But we very well know her name is Mrs. Langston," Lady Hartworth said.

"Mama! You are not to ever repeat that—and I pray that you never, ever reveal anything you read in Mrs. Langston's letters."

The mother looked like she'd found a shiny guinea. "You said her name!"

Georgiana gave a resigned shrug.

"I believe my brother entrusted his papers into your daughter's care because he could depend upon her discretion," Alex said. "He was a most private person."

"Then I won't tell anyone about that bit o' muslin's shockingly bold letters to the late duke."

"Those letters, I believe, were written before my

brother had the good sense to ask for Lady Georgiana's hand. Thereafter, he was besotted over no one save your beautiful daughter."

Her ladyship's eyes widened. "I forgot to note the date on the letters. May I look just once again?" Her gaze lifted to Georgiana.

"No."

"You see, your grace, how she treats me."

"She's an exceedingly caring daughter, and well you know it."

"I will concede that to her."

"Now Mama, why do you not return to your chamber and finish writing your letters?"

"Allow me to walk you there," Alex said.

"I shan't send a chaperon to the library," the dowager announced, peering up at the duke with laughing eyes. "I hope you can manage to compromise my daughter."

"Mama!" Georgiana shrieked.

"But, dearest, I wouldn't say that to anyone except Hamford."

"Fordham," Georgiana corrected, then turned to him. "Pray, your grace, do *not* listen to my mother. I am mortified."

"If it were in my nature to compromise a lady," he said to the mother, "I can think of no worthier candidate than your daughter."

"Fordham!"Georgiana gave him a scornful look.

Once they got her mother settled, they moved to the library and closed the door, Georgiana was all eagerness. "Have you seen Mrs. Langston?"

"Many times. The first time was when I was eighteen. She was Hamlet's Ophelia." He enjoyed teasing Georgiana.

"That is not what I meant. Have you spoken to her?"

"Oh, most certainly. I asked her if she killed her former lover. She denied it, of course."

Georgiana's eyes narrowed. "You jest."

He met her gaze and was powerless not to smile. "I went to see the lady yesterday afternoon."

When no further comments were communicated, she asked, "You went to her house?"

"Yes."

"And you went by yourself?"

"Oh, yes. Much more intimate, more conducive to a free exchange, do you not think?"

"It depends. Did she mention your strong resemblance to Freddie?"

"Oh, yes. Only she said I was . . . now let me see, did she say I was more manly or more muscular? It doesn't signify." He loved dragging this out, loved trying to see if he could make her jealous.

"And what chamber did you meet her in?"

"It wasn't her bedchamber, if that's what you're thinking."

She put hands to hips and gave him a shocked expression. "I thought no such thing."

"The woman could not have looked more respectable. If I hadn't known better, I would never have thought she could be any man's mistress."

"Did you find her . . . pretty?"

"Almost as pretty as I thought her when I was eighteen." Which was not quite the truth—though her demeanor made her prettier than he had first thought upon seeing her yesterday.

"Well, then, did you learn if she had come to loathe Freddie after her dismissed her?"

The time for jesting was over. "She's still in love

with him. Have you read her letters to Freddie yet?"

"No. I had to school myself not to allow myself to read them before I've sorted all the correspondence and organized them by dates—which I have not yet finished doing."

He smirked. "So you're saving the juicy letters for a reward?"

She hung her head. "I confess I am."

He chuckled. "By the way, while you're shuffling through these papers, I should like the receipt for the Rafael. Since I'm eliminating so many suspects, I can't leave any stone unturned. It's not likely some deranged art lover would kill to obtain the Rafael, but I ought to give a go at looking into it."

"If you're interested in who handled the sale, I can tell you it was Mr. Christie on King Street."

"That's what I needed."

"I should like to return to the discussion of a certain actress. What makes you think she still considered herself in love with Freddie? Has she not a new protector?"

"She has, but on the night she learned of Freddie's death, she was unable to perform. She said yesterday was the first day she could mention his name without launching into tears." Would such knowledge make Georgiana feel guilty? She certainly hadn't loved Freddie that fiercely. Had she? Was she *that* good at disguising her emotions? He watched her for a reaction.

Her lengthy lashes lowered, and she swallowed. Then, with a defiant shrug, she met his gaze head on. "Many a scorned woman is responsible for killing a man she loved. There's that if-I-can't-have-him-no-one-will mentality."

"She's not like that."

There was fire in Georgiana's coffee-colored eyes when she spoke. "And you could tell this after a single meeting?"

"As well as I could dismiss my cousin and other suspects."

"Then, your grace, it must come back to you. You had the most to gain from Freddie's death." He'd never seen her angrier.

For one lightning bolt second he wanted to force a searing kiss upon her and coax her into admitting she did not suspect him, but his anger won out. "If that's the way you feel, I have no more to say." He turned his back on her and stormed from the chamber.

* * *

When the duke strode from the library, she had started after him, but in his rage, he did not hear her footsteps, and she was too proud to call out. Long after he was gone she still trembled. How she wished she could take back her insensitive words. She hadn't even meant them.

She meant only to emphasize that his inquiries were getting nowhere, that he was too trusting. He needed to develop an impermeable callousness. But now, it seemed, his callousness was only toward her.

For the next several days, he absented himself for Hartworth House. Nothing could have better succeeded in making her crave his companionship. She'd not known how much she had looked forward to his visits until they ceased. Each day she and Angelique would contrive to dress her person and her hair beautifully in the hopes that Fordham would come. Each time she heard a horse or a carriage in the square, she'd run to the window, only to walk away disappointed.

He was not coming back.

She devised a thousand scenarios in which she lured him to return, but when it came to implementing them, she could not. Perhaps it was better this way. The reigning Duke of Fordham had a most unsettling influence on her. He brought out a wantonness she had not known she possessed.

Nor did she want to possess such a deviant trait!

The monotony of her days would have been unbearable were it not for Mrs. Langston's heartbreakingly lovely letters to Freddie. Georgiana had finally sorted through and organized all of Freddie's papers, and she began by reading those written by Freddie's former mistress.

Even after reading just the first letter, Georgiana was inclined to agree with Fordham's assessment of the actress's innocence. These were not obligatory letters written by a courtesan to the man who provided handsomely for her. These were written with a love so overwhelming, reading them brought tears to Georgiana's eyes.

When you are at Gosingham, it's as if my whole existence is snuffed. I am only alive when I'm with you, my darling Freddie. I cannot conceive how you can be so happy in the country whilst I am in London for I can never be happy when we are separated.

I would give up the stage, my house, my last semblance of pride to be able to spend every day with you, every night in your arms.

Whether Georgiana's tears were for poor Mrs.

Langston's misery or for her own guilt that she'd never loved Freddie so passionately, she could not say.

Most of the letters appeared to have been written during Freddie's frequent trips to Gosingham and revealed a woman tormented with love. A few were obviously written to him in London, begging him not to go away.

You are too cruel to me. Just last week you returned from a whole month at Gosingham, and now you propose to return! I can count on the fingers of one hand the number of nights you have shared my bed in the last two months. You really are too unfeeling toward me. I cannot bear it. Please, I beg you, stay longer.

In another letter she wrote *No man has ever been loved with the potency with which I love you. I shall go to my grave loving you.*

For the most part, there was nothing offensive to a maiden in the letters. The closest Georgiana came to blushing was when Mrs. Langston alluded to a night in which she and Freddie had made love multiple times. *I wish I knew what magical ingredient was responsible for your ardor last night, my dearest love, for I would ensure you received large doses of it every day. No night has ever given me greater pleasure. Even as I write this, I wish you were lying beside me, I wish I could feel you inside me.*

When Georgiana read this, she felt a tingling low in her torso. And she thought about Fordham. Why was it he and only he had ever affected her in that profoundly physical way?

She came to the last of Mrs. Langston's letters with a deep disappointment. She had looked forward to reading them since the day she'd received the first bundle, and now she would no longer have that eager anticipation.

Also, it felt almost like saying good-bye to a friend, for—like Fordham—Georgiana had come to admire Mrs. Langston and her constancy toward Freddie. The actress's last letter was vastly different from the others:

Had you torn out my heart and tossed it on the racecourse at Newmarket to be trampled, I could not experience a greater pain that what you have dealt me. The loss of your affections is worse than death. And worse than the loss of your affections is the humiliation I feel. You've seen fit to hand me over to Sir Arthur as if I'm a common whore at Covent Garden.

A woman this angry is a woman who could commit murder.

I must tell Fordham.

$\mathcal{C}$hapter 14

Only with the greatest restraint was Georgiana able to stop herself from racing to Fordham House to apprise his grace of her newest suspicion. Given that it was already night, it wasn't likely he'd even be there. But that wasn't the reason that had kept her away. She was cognizant of just how acutely she wished to see him, and such knowledge made her ashamed. She had never been so eager to see the man with whom she had pledged to spend her life.

It did not feel right to so thoroughly crave being with the brother of her betrothed. None of these physical reactions the new duke elicited in her felt right. Since he'd stolen that kiss she ought not to want to see him ever again, but she seemed powerless to deprive herself of his company.

Even if he were home, she would not go there. He would believe she had come because she couldn't bear not seeing him. The man was far too convinced of his charms. It was well known that he captured female hearts with the same regularity other men acquired snuff boxes.

She went to the writing table and wrote a short missive to him.

Your Grace,
Whilst reading your brother's correspondence I have come across a letter which I believe could

establish a motive for wishing to kill Freddie.
Should you wish to see it, you might come by
Hartworth House.
Lady G.

Before she had sealed the letter, she had
considered apologizing to him for her accusations,
but she decided against it. If he came, she would
tell him to his face. With sincerity. But not now.
She did not want to divert his attention from the
true purpose of her letter.

She only hoped she did not sound pitiable.

* * *

It was his first letter from her. Alex thought he
would have been able to attribute the penmanship
to her from among a hundred offerings for it
conveyed her persona. The letters lacked the
flourishes and frills of other females' efforts—just
like her. Simple, yet unmistakably feminine.

He was relieved to receive her letter. He had
determined not to go to her. The woman was
maddening. Her effect upon him was maddening.
He was better off not seeing her. Only he wasn't.
He'd been away from her for four days now. Four
days of hungering for her. Four days of torture.

Now he had a plausible excuse for seeing her.

"When did this letter arrive?" he asked his
butler.

"Last night, your grace, just after you went
out."

"Good." Alex would go to her after he shaved
and dressed. He could only hope that she had
been eagerly awaiting him since early last evening.

As Gates shaved him, Alex's thoughts were on
Georgiana. Was it possible she was missing him
as much as he was missing her? She was as

difficult to read as an untried two-year-old filly, and he'd always prided himself on his ability to understand women. That was one of the reasons he'd never been in want of affectionate females.

He directed his thoughts back to the subject of the letter she'd written him. To whom could she be referring? He really was at a loss to imagine which member of that shooting party could wish Freddie dead—other than Sir Arthur, who would, quite naturally, be jealous of Freddie. A mere baronet unfavorably compared in every measure to a youthful duke of great fortune—but most of all in the affections of a lady adored by the baronet.

But Alex had read Sir Arthur's letters. Alex had talked with the man about Freddie. And Alex was convinced of the man's innocence.

That was the problem. Alex didn't think any of those men guilty of the calculated murder of his brother. Was he too trusting? Too easily swayed? He would soon learn something that might help in his quest to apprehend Freddie's killer.

* * *

As soon as he was shown into the Hartworth library and his eyes met Georgiana's, she favored him with a smile. Never before had she greeted him in so friendly a fashion. Georgiana's rarely bestowed smiles, with her snowy white, perfectly formed teeth, were something out of the ordinary. It made him feel like an inexperienced schoolboy facing his first love.

He was nearly undone when she walked up to him, that radiant smile never dimming, her faint rose scent almost unleashing his passion. God, but she was beautiful! She wore the same muted rose gown she was wearing the night of their kiss

Why was it he could remember her wardrobe—even the faded togs she'd worn when he'd first met her—when he'd never before noticed women's clothing?

"First, your grace, I must apologize to you. It was unpardonable for me to lash out at you as I did last week. I beg that you realize I do not now nor have I ever believed you guilty of murdering Freddie." She extended her hands, and when he reached out, she covered his with hers. "Can you forgive me?"

It might just be a hand clasp, but to him—hungering for her as he did—it was erotic. He cocked his head and strived for flippancy. "Were I a murderer, my lady, I daresay you'd have been strangled."

Her lips pursed, but she could not suppress a smile "I am told I can be most provoking."

He laughed but could not gallantly deny that she was, indeed, excessively provoking. "Now tell me about the murderer."

"Come sit on the sofa. You can read it for yourself."

To his surprise, she sat next to him and gave him the letter. It was a second before he realized it was not the letter that smelled so sweetly of roses. It was the woman beside him. He looked quickly to the signature, though he already knew from the handwriting it was penned by a woman. *Sophia Langston.*

Did she have a strong motive for Freddie's death? He found it difficult to believe. He proceeded to read the letter, then dropped it in his lap and faced her.

"A woman most thoroughly scorned, would you not agree?" Georgiana asked, somberly.

"I will own she was furious when she wrote this."

Georgiana's brows lowered. "I'm anticipating a *but* in your voice."

He nodded. "If you'd met the woman you'd know she was incapable of murdering Freddie."

"It's unlikely she'd affect me as profoundly as she's affected you. I'm a female."

"What does that mean?"

"You were obviously taken in by her charms."

"What kind of charms would you be referring to?"

She hesitated a moment before answering. "The woman's a vixen!"

"Do you honestly believe that after reading her letters? Did you not come to believe the depth of her devotion to my brother?"

"I will own she was deeply in love with him. She did not sound like I would imagine a doxy would sound."

He nodded in agreement.

"And here's *my* but," she said. "You and I agreed at the outset of this . . . this inquiry into Freddie's death that there were two reasons to commit murder. The first is for financial gain."

"One is obliged to point to me there."

"But of course you didn't do it," she conceded.

He eyed her, nodding. "The other reason's for love."

"Exactly."

He shook his head. "She didn't do it."

Her eyes narrowed. "So we're back to that. You're her champion. Did she lure you? Is she to become your mistress?"

"She did not, and she is not." He wasn't about to tell Georgiana that Sophia Langston was twice as old as she and half as pretty.

She looked askance at him. "Can you honestly tell me you were immune to her charms?"

"Are you're jealous, Georgiana?"

Fire lit her eyes. "*Lady* Georgiana. I told you *not* to address me in such a manner."

"Yes, I recall," he said in a low, husky voice, "the night we kissed."

"The night *you* kissed!"

"Yes, I did. You're a very good kisser, Georgiana."

She issued a deep sigh of exasperation. "How did we get onto this odious topic of conversation?"

"There's nothing odious about kissing you, but I believe the conversation diverged to this topic when I accused you of being jealous of Mrs. Langston."

"You're incredibly odious."

"But thankfully not a murderer. Now we're back on topic."

"I shouldn't have sent you that letter."

"In all seriousness, my lady, you needed to. I appreciate your eagerness to help the investigation into the death of my brother, your betrothed. As you've attempted to instill in me, we cannot ignore any lead. And while I don't believe Sophia Langston capable of having murdered or having instigated the murder of Freddie, I shall not ignore the lead."

"What will you do?"

He thought for a moment before answering. "Part of my conviction of her innocence hinges upon her telling me that when she learned of Freddie's death she was too prostrate with grief to perform that night."

"You'll find out if she was telling you the

truth?"

"Yes. And furthermore I will have my man—he's most resourceful—befriend someone in Mrs. Langston's household to see if she could have made the journey to Gosingham—though that would have been difficult, given that the length of that trip would prevent her from being on stage for a week."

"How could you find out if she encouraged someone else to do it?"

He shrugged. "I shall have to think on that."

"I am gratified that you're at least amenable to suspecting *someone* of the vile deed."

"I didn't actually say I suspected her, but as you've frequently pointed out, I should not be so easily convinced of innocence. I still cannot conceive that any of those who knew Freddie could be guilty."

"You do seem to have exonerated—at least in your mind—most members of the shooting party."

He started to count on his fingers. "My cousin, most certainly. Freddie's best friend as well. I do not believe Sir Arthur guilty, either." He looked her in the eye. "I'm equally convinced of the innocence of Mrs. Langston."

"Are you sure you weren't captivated by her beauty?"

He did not remove his pensive gaze from her. "I'm sure."

He thought perhaps she let out a barely audible sigh. "You've left off your Gosingham neighbor."

"I have difficulty believing Lord Barnstaple would wish his lifelong friend dead, but I'm willing to explore any motives that should arise." He couldn't shake the question of Barnstaple asking Freddie for the additional land by the lake. To his knowledge, Freddie had never consented. "And I haven't ruled out Lord Hickington either," he added.

Her brows lowered. "What possible motive could Lord Hickington have for wishing Freddie dead?"

Alex's lazy gaze moved from the perfection of her face, to her lovely shoulders, to skim along the smooth curves of her slender body. "You."

Her mouth dropped open. "Whatever can you mean?"

"Can you deny that the man has asked for your hand?"

"That was a long time ago."

"And he's still unwed. Does he not seem to be anxiously seeking your company?"

"I am sure the silly man would not resort to murder to win my hand. In fact there's nothing he could do that would gain my affections."

"I'm happy to know that, Georgiana."

"I have asked you to cease trying to make love to me."

"Acknowledge you've missed me."

"Wretched man."

She did not deny having missed him. He stood and smiled down at her. "Alas, I must go instruct my man to spy on Mrs. Langston."

He hoped the brevity of his visit would ignite her desire to see him again. Soon.

Disappointment from leaving her now was easily worth the reward of her smiling welcome when next he returned.

* * *

Not long after Alex gave Gates his orders—whilst also having the good man make inquiries at Drury Lane—Alex was surprised to find Barnstaple calling on him.

They met in the library, which was altogether different from the cozy library at Hartworth House where he'd kissed Georgiana. The Fordham library was especially grand for the modest proportions of a town house. It featured no less than two fireplaces, a vast number of Doric columns, and an even more vast number of leather-bound books. He invited his Lincolnshire neighbor to sit on one of the chamber's four sofas.

"I called yesterday," Barnstaple said, "but when you weren't here I was happy to visit with your charming sisters." He sighed. "I needed to offer them my condolences on Freddie's death. Such a sad occurrence, to be sure."

Alex's expression grave, he nodded, then changed the topic. "It's a wonder I didn't see you at White's last night." Alex had continued going to his brother's club in the hopes of picking up something that might help lead to his brother's killer. Sir Arthur had been there, and Alex had once more engaged him in conversation but still believed the man innocent.

"I was fatigued. I'd just arrived in London late in the afternoon. I had a very early night.

Nothing's more tiring than traveling all day in a coach, do you not agree?"

"I do, and I'm flattered that you came straight away to Fordham House."

"I felt I had an obligation to see your sisters. You see, I hadn't written them since Freddie's tragic death. Thought I'd visit them in person to tell them how dearly I cherished my friendship with their brother."

"Very kind of you."

"There's another matter I wish to speak to you about."

Would he bring up the land adjacent to Gosingham? Alex arched a brow.

"Freddie had verbally given me permission to acquire a small parcel of your land, but he died before we could complete the transaction."

Alex's attention perked. The only letter in Freddie's papers mentioning the land expressly said Freddie had refused to convey the property to his neighbor. Now that Freddie was dead, there was only Barnstaple's word for it that Freddie had agreed to part with the parcel.

Though Alex was not close to Freddie, he knew his brother was more interested in expanding his land holdings than in selling them off. God knows he didn't need the money. Of course, there was the longstanding—though not terribly close—friendship between the two neighbors. Perhaps Freddie was willing to part with the land in consideration of their friendship.

"Freddie said nothing to me about this," Alex responded. "It would have been something he'd have directed to the attention of our solicitor. Have you checked with Waterman?"

"No. You see, Freddie just agreed at the shooting party. I hardly think he would yet have forwarded it to Waterman."

"So, my dear fellow, am I correct in thinking you've come to ask me to approve the conveyance of this property to you?"

Barnstaple nodded.

"And what piece of property would this be?"

"It's a little parcel between my modest property and the smaller of the Fordham lakes Capability Brown built for your father. I wouldn't even think of asking were it not that you already have the larger lake."

"So then you'd be able to enjoy having a lake on your property without the cursed nuisance and expense of having one dug? Is that correct?"

Alex was well aware of the vast sums his father had paid to have the previously barren land surrounding Gosingham transformed with man-made hills and lakes as well as trees brought in from as far away as North America.

"Yes, but as I said, I'm willing to pay."

"Wretched luck Freddie died before he could instruct Waterman to draw up the contracts." If, indeed, such an agreement had even been reached between the two men. "The pity of it is that my father's dying instructions were that no part of our land was ever to be sold or given away. It wasn't like Freddie to go against our parent's wishes."

"You know how it is with one's parents. They say so many things that were never meant to be taken literally. Take my father, may he rest in peace. He told us that he was exceedingly attached to the Gainsborough of his sister—one of two, I might add—and he did not want it to leave the family. I don't mind saying I sold it for an enormous sum after the old fellow died. I think he would have done the same, given the offer." He shrugged. "It's not as if we don't have another portrait of Aunt Fanny—just as you have another lake."

"Some men do value money above all other things, but not the men in my family, I regret to tell you."

Lord Barnstaple's face fell, and it was a moment before he spoke. "Does this mean you will not honor the agreement between your brother and me?"

"Not at all, dear fellow. You've only to show me proof of the agreement, and I will be honor bound to comply with it."

Barnstaple stood and glared at Alex. "I can't believe you could be unmoved by our long-standing friendship."

"You can always count on me as a friend, my dear Lord Barnstaple, but I have a duty to honor my own father's request above yours. This is not to say that you're not welcome to use the small lake at any time you wish."

Barnstaple murmured thanks as he nodded. "I shall not take this refusal to sell as your final answer. I pray you'll reconsider, your grace." Lord Barnstaple swept from the room.

Finally! Alex had a bona fide suspect in

his Lincolnshire neighbor. Until today he would never have thought his old neighbor capable of killing Freddie. Now he had a strong motive, though for the life of him, Alex could not understand why it was so blasted important to Barnstaple that he acquire a slender strip of land. Furthermore, Alex knew his neighbor's pockets were shallow. He couldn't possibly be prepared to pay very much for that lake access. Had he hoped to barter using the two familyies' high regard for one another?

Even though Alex had heretofore been trusting of the members of the shooting party, he did not believe Barnstaple. Freddie would never have consented to give away any of the Fordham holdings—even for friendship.

Two questions were posed. Why was a slip of land so important to Barnstaple, and why would it be worth killing for? Alex could not deny that Capability Brown had outdone even his own enormous talents when he'd designed the small lake. Spanned by a humpback bridge made of the local stone, the shimmering body of water reflected the graceful lines of a small Grecian temple constructed on a Brown-created hill covered in velvety grass. Willows bent to dust the water on the opposite side. A prettier place Alex had never seen.

He could understand coveting such a place—though such a vice was alien to him— but killing for it? Unimaginable.

Still, this was his most solid lead yet. If the killer should prove to be Barnstaple, though, how could Alex prove it? Obviously, there were no witnesses, and expecting his neighbor to confess was unrealistic.

Establishing guilt would be nearly impossible.

Now Alex pondered if he should apprise Georgiana of this newest development. Perhaps he should wait a few days, see what the valet learned about Mrs. Langston. Then when he reported to Georgiana, he would have much to reveal.

Hopefully, another prolonged absence would elicit the lady's provocative smile. And perhaps even unfurl some of her tightly guarded affections.

$\mathcal{C}$hapter 15

When Georgiana first started listening to Lady Wycliff speak on expanding the franchise at the next Tuesday gathering, she was possessed of the oddest feeling that she didn't belong there. It wasn't just that she felt vastly inferior to the exceedingly intelligent and well-informed Lady Wycliff—which she most decidedly did. It was more that she felt as out of place as she would had she wandered into a gathering of Hottentots.

No peer or peeress of Georgiana's acquaintance had ever dared to criticize their own class or the system of government by which they were ruled. Georgiana showed great restraint in not leaping up to protest. How could anyone think *everyone* had the right to vote? Surely illiterate men had no use casting a ballot. What kind of men would be elected if *everyone* had their say in an election?

She couldn't help but remember what went on in France just two decades previously. Such wild thinking could bring about the end of the aristocratic class. Unconsciously, she clasped a delicate hand around her cambric collar.

She conceded that Lady Wycliff was possessed of uncommon intelligence. "It's a pity," Lady Wycliff said, "the British cannot learn from the American Mr. Jefferson, who has written that all men are created equal. Here men who are not freeholders are not considered worthy to vote." The lovely lady, dressed in an exquisite pale blue muslin dress, paused, eyeing each woman seated in gilt chairs forming a ring around her. "It is wrong."

Georgiana was stunned. Lady Wycliff was, after all, the wife of an earl. In addition to being exposed to thinking so alien to everything she had ever heard in her four-and-twenty years, Georgiana sighed at her own lack of knowledge. To be truthful, she had never heard of the American Mr. Jefferson. How did one like Lord Wycliff's beautiful wife acquire such knowledge?

The more Georgiana listened, the more she admired Lady Wycliff's magnanimity to the masses. Georgiana bore no ill will to the illiterate. She had even on occasion helped to teach the unwashed young girls at the school Mama sponsored. She had knitted gloves to keep their little hands warm, and had also presented her glove work to the family's coachman, over whom she worried on cold days. She had begged her Papa to increase the meager wage he paid his servants, though her pleas had fallen on deaf ears. She had wept at the sight of hungry, barefoot young orphans in the Capital and had spent her entire quarter's allowance in feeding and clothing dozens of these children.

While she might not be possessed of the knowledge of Lady Wycliff, she equaled her in compassion. But caring for the masses and considering them *equals* were two completely different matters. Was that Mr. Jefferson delusional?

Anyone who was not blind could observe the advantages of a man like the Duke of Fordham and see how vastly different he was from a ragged chestnut hawker on The Strand. No one could ever think them equal. Yet, if she understood what Lady Wycliff was promulgating, both men should be extended the right to vote.

It was such a novel idea that it was impossible for Georgiana to accept such a far-fetched scheme.

Though Georgiana had little interest in politics, she found herself wishing to be more educated on such matters. Though, of course, she would never sympathize with those Whigs.

* * *

Harry Wycliff quietly entered Alex's library. The Fordham butler had instructions that Wycliff's and Sinjin's cards were not ever to be presented. Those two old friends were always to be shown straight away to whatever chamber Alex occupied.

Alex looked up over the top of his *Morning Chronicle*. "Ah! It's Tuesday. Your good lady has thrown you out."

"Yes and no." Harry came to sit on the sofa closest to his friend. "Today she's actually asked that I speak at the end of the meeting, and I'm going to make you come with me."

"What topic are you to address?"

"Louisa's discussing expanding the franchise today and wants me to more thoroughly explain just who is allowed to vote. She thought having a Member of Parliament there would give more credit to her Tuesday gathering, and she encouraged me to bring other MPs."

Alex playfully lowered his brows. "Before you wed Lady Wycliff, did you not poke shameful fun at her bluestocking friends?"

He chuckled. "I can hardly admit that now that your worthy sister has joined the group."

Alex nodded thoughtfully. "Freddie was not happy when he learned Margaret was casting her support to the Whigs."

"Then I expect he nearly had apoplexy when you became a Whig."

"Fortunately, Freddie was possessed of a mild manner."

"Speaking of your brother, how go your inquiries?"

"Poorly—until last night."

Harry's brows arched.

"It's not much, but I may have found a motive." He moved to the sofa across from where Harry sat and proceeded to tell Lord Wycliff of Lord Barnstaple's suspicious behavior.

"I agree," Harry said. "It sounds damned suspicious, but how in the devil can you ever prove it, were he to be the killer? It's not as if there were any witnesses, and the bloody man's not likely to confess."

"I suppose I shall have to beat a confession out of him," Alex said drolly.

"A pity you can't."

"There's another possible suspect. Lady Georgiana, who's mad to help in these inquiries, is convinced that Freddie's dismissal of Sophia Langston sent the actress into a murdering frenzy."

"Did Freddie not make a generous settlement on Mrs. Langston?"

Alex nodded. "An exceedingly generous settlement."

"And is she not now under the protection of Sir Arthur?"

"She is, but there's a letter she wrote to Freddie in which she voiced her humiliation at being tossed to another man as if she were a common doxy."

"And I perceive Lady Georgiana has seen this letter?" Sun streaming in the nearly window caused Harry to squint as he spoke.

Alex rose and went to draw the celery-coloured velvet draperies closest to Harry.

"Yes."

A grin on his face, Harry eyed him. "And how go things with you and Lady Georgiana?"

"I don't know to what you're referring. Do not forget the lady was betrothed to my late brother, and don't forget Freddie and I had vastly different taste in women."

Harry cocked a brow, a mischievous grin on his face. "I understand she's not wearing mourning for him."

"Lady Georgiana is unlike other women. One should not judge her by conventional measurements. Her decision to wear no mourning has nothing to do with the degree of her affection for Freddie and everything to do with her abhorrence of ducal hangers-on."

"So she didn't feel right passing herself off as a member of the Haversham/Fordham family since she had not actually married your brother?"

"Correct."

"Admirable, I should think."

"Yes."

"Louisa told me she expected Lady Georgiana to attend today's gathering."

"That's what my sister said. It surprised me, given that the Marquesses of Hartworth have always been so strongly associated with Tories, and I believe she, too, sympathizes with them."

Harry stood. "Then we must help convince her otherwise."

Alex left his desk. "Is Sinjin coming?"

Wycliff's brows lowered. "What do you think?"

"Since his charming wife is as passionate over civil liberties as is your wife, I expect she's persuaded him to come. You two are very lucky." Alex doubted he would ever find a wife half as compatible—or as loving—as the ones Harry and Sinjin had found.

* * *

The three lords previously of Eton, along with Lord Wycliff's cousin, Edward Coke, who'd had the misfortune of having attended Harrow, reached the Wycliff drawing room a few minutes before Lady Wycliff wrapped up her comments. At first Alex stood at the chamber's doorway, surveying the gathering. Gilt side chairs formed a circle facing the speaker. Georgiana sat next to his sister.

He strode to the back of the room, took an unclaimed gilt chair, and moved to place it between Margaret and Georgiana. His sister looked up and smiled at him. Georgiana scowled, which is exactly what he had expected of her. He'd spent enough time in her company to accurately predict what she was going to do—much of the time.

He almost spoke to her, but that would be discourteous to Lady Wycliff. Better to wait until she finished.

"One last comment," Lady Wycliff said, "though this is actually the subject for another program, but while we're examining our country's electioneering, I propose that everyone in this chamber—including our right honorable Members of Parliament—consider the merits of a secret ballot and the prohibition of bribing voters."

While most of the ladies nodded approvingly, Georgiana did not. From the shocked expression on her face, Alex thought she may never before have heard of such a thing as a secret ballot.

"And now," Lady Wycliff concluded, "I have asked Lord Wycliff to enumerate our country's qualifications for voters. He has also said he will do us the goodness of answering any questions we ladies might have."

It only took Harry a moment to sketch out the qualifications for both candidates and voters, then he proceeded to field questions.

"So," Alex whispered to Georgiana, "I perceive you are shocked at the notion of a secret ballot."

She lowered her voice. "Indeed I am! I've never contemplated such a thing. Do you not agree one must be held accountable for one's actions?"

"In most cases, yes, but - - -"

The bespectacled older woman at Georgiana's left spun around, glared, and shushed him.

He and Georgiana exchanged amused looks, and he shrugged. He planned to continue the conversation when Harry stopped talking, but by then everyone was milling about, and Sinjin and Coke were speaking to him, then Coke's little blonde wife came up to Alex. "Your grace, it was so very kind of you to pay back the money you borrowed from Edward—with such interest! We're exceedingly grateful. We've been able to purchase a house just around the corner from here—all thanks to you."

"It's I who am grateful. Your husband advanced me the money at a time when I was in desperate need." Desperate might be a bit too strong a word, but at the time it had been very important that he secure the loan in order to win his seat in the House of Commons. He'd patched together several donors, but when the bills were settled, he hadn't enough without the loan from Edward Coke.

He returned his attention to Georgiana, who stared at him as if he's just sprouted a pair of horns.

"Really, my lady, there is much to recommend secret ballots," he said.

His sister moved closer and hooked her arm to his. "Indeed there is, Lady Georgiana. We must strive to convince you." Margaret turned to him. "Do ride back with us. It's your coach, after all. You and I can try to sway the lady."

He eyed Georgiana. "I consider it my mission."

There was a coolness about her that he hadn't seen since that first week.

* * *

It wasn't the prospect of a secret ballot that had deprived Georgiana of the ability to smile. It was Ellie Coke's comment about the loan Fordham had received from her husband *before* Freddie's death. That gave Freddie's younger brother a much stronger motive to commit murder. She'd not known that before he inherited a prosperous dukedom, the new duke been *desperate* for money.

That knowledge sent her insides sinking and her exterior shaking. Was he so desperate for money that he would kill his own brother?

In the coach on the way home, he faced her. Even fearing him as she did at that moment, the sight of his finely chiseled face, the playful curl of his mouth, and the memory of their searing kiss, sent her heartbeat strumming.

"So what does our little Tory sympathizer think of expanding the voting base?" he asked.

She glared at him. "I am not *your* little anything."

He turned to the sister who sat beside him. "My lady thinks it's unfair to our dead brother for her to be pleasant to his successor."

Sweet-tempered Margaret smiled at Georgiana. "As much as I grieve my brother's passing, I can truthfully say there's never been a better Duke of Fordham than my youngest brother. Not even our dear father." She shrugged. "I know it might seem too early to tell, but I know Alex. I've known him since the moment of my birth. All his predecessors were Tories who cared more for increasing their own worth than they cared for Humanity. Alex is the most altruistic man I've ever known. It was only natural for a man like him to turn his back on the Tories."

He rolled his eyes and directed his attention to Georgiana. "I daresay my sister's both drunk on Whig principles and blinded by devotion to the brother who defended her against our two elder brothers."

"I am not blind. Can you deny that before you left Gosingham—just the day after you succeeded—you gave instructions that a school must be set up to teach every lad and every girl? The cottagers' children as well as the children of every servant at Gosingham?"

He gave a casual shrug. "A small thing to do. I mean to do it at the other seven estates belonging to the Duke of Fordham." He turned to Georgiana. "Do you not think the distribution of wealth in our country is embarrassing? Is it not ridiculous that I am the possessor of eight estates, a town house in London, and a shooting lodge in Scotland while so many of our countrymen have no home?"

"But that's the way it's always been," Georgiana defended.

"And the Whigs and the Radicals are all about change, change that will afford *all* our countrymen rights—rights to vote, rights to be educated, rights to form labor unions to demand a decent wage."

Georgiana could not argue with such noble sentiment. "How did someone from your background come to embrace such ideals?"

He shrugged. "It started with Sinjin, Lord Slade. Since he was a lad, he was the most honest, noble person I've ever known. He encouraged me to stand for the House of Commons. I resisted at first. Because of him, I began to read. Jeremy Bentham. Thomas Paine. Philip Lewis's essays. Like Sinjin, I came to realize the old way of doing things was wrong. Change was needed."

"So you converted to a Whig, stood for office, and won," Georgiana said. She was starting to thaw. Everything he'd said since joining her in the coach convinced her of his good heart. How could such a man ever contemplate murder?

But still, he had a powerful motive. That motive, though, was even more powerful now that she knew he meant to use his new wealth to accomplish what he'd been passionately fighting for in Parliament—to help the less fortunate.

She had never felt more confused. Ever since she'd sat in the Wycliffs' drawing room that morning, she'd felt as if her four-and-twenty years had all been a huge deception. Were all these people right and generations of Fenton/Hartworths nothing more than selfish despots?

Was Fordham truly the noble man he projected, or was he a cold-blooded murderer?

"And now I've lost my hard-fought seat in Commons to sit in the House of Lords."

"Tell me," Georgiana said, "if I were interested in learning more of political matters, which authors should I read? I confess to feeling most inadequate in the presence of the ladies who gather at Wycliff House on Tuesdays."

Lady Margaret answered. "Do you not think she should start with Mr. Lewis's essays?"

Fordham nodded. "A good suggestion, Maggie. They wonderfully distill the great thinkers of our generation."

"They're in a book?" Georgiana asked.

He shook his head. "No. You'll find them in the *Edinburgh Review.*"

"I don't know that my brother subscribes," Georgiana said.

Fordham chuckled. "I doubt that he does."

"There's nothing to prevent you from subscribing," Lady Margaret suggested.

Georgiana nodded. "A capital idea."

When they drew up in front of her house, the duke said, "If I learn of anything about . . . that Drury Lane situation, my lady, I shall contact you."

She realized he didn't want his sister to know about the investigation into Freddie's death. Drury Lane obviously referred to the theatre where Mrs. Langston trod the boards. "It's very good of you, your grace, though I do think it's too soon after Freddie's death for us to go to the theatre. Much too frivolous."

A grin pinched his tanned cheeks. "You are, of course, right. Might I offer to bring you some of my copies of the *Edinburgh Review*?"

"That would be very kind of you."

As conflicted as she was, something within her tingled with excitement at the prospect of him calling upon her.

$\mathcal{C}$hapter 16

Unlike other valets who had first served as batman to a gentleman officer and whose manners weren't fit for a drawing room, Gates effortlessly adapted to his roles so convincingly other servants in the household looked up at him as if he were a nobleman who'd been switched at birth. These qualities enabled the young man to penetrate the circle of female domestics at Mrs. Langston's house as easily as a fluffy kitten. Indeed, Alex had no doubts that those female servants would have done anything legal to gain the handsome young valet's favor.

Within three days Gates had ingratiated himself with the Langston staff, satisfactorily completed his mission, and returned to report to his master.

A serious look on his lightly freckled face as he studied his master, Gates did not bring up the subject of his recent absence. Alex knew he was waiting to be asked.

"So, my good man," Alex said when the impeccably dressed Gates appeared first thing in the morning to shave his master, "have you learned if Mrs. Langston has undertaken any journeys?"

"She has not, your grace. Her servants say that in the last year—coinciding with the time her connection to the late duke was severed—she has only left the house to go to Drury Lane."

"And has she had gentlemen callers, other than Sir Arthur?"

"None whatsoever—except, I was told, the new Duke of Fordham."

It was really quite amazing how thoroughly servants kept up with their masters' private affairs. "You have verified my instincts about the lady." Unless she and Sir Arthur had concocted an unlikely scheme to murder Freddie, the lady was innocent.

"It's the opinion of the servants," Gates said, "one and all, that she's been rather pining away since the duke broke with her."

"And your Drury Lane investigation?" Alex asked when the hot cloth was removed from his face.

"She's noted for never missing a night—save one night a few weeks ago. She sent a missive to the theatre, saying she could not go on because she could not stop crying after being notified of the death of someone to whom she had been very close."

"You've done an excellent job of confirming everything I suspected," Alex said, dismissing his man.

Before he shared this information with Georgiana, Alex had one last avenue of inquiry to consider. He would talk to Mr. Christie and find out if there was another eager bidder for the Rafael Freddie had recently purchased.

* * *

The stately white stone building on King Street looked like an establishment that would deal in fine works of art. Alex's opinion was only reinforced when he entered the building. The first thing he saw on a stark white wall was a large full-length portrait of a beautiful woman with great mounds of powdered hair. An unmistakable Gainsborough. Alex found himself wondering if it might be the portrait of Lord Barnstaple's Aunt Fanny.

An impeccably dressed aging gentleman approached him. "Your grace, allow me to say how honored I am to see you again."

Alex was quite certain he'd never before seen this man, but then he realized the man must be mistaking him for Freddie. "I daresay you've confused me with my recently deceased brother, Frederick, the eighth Duke of Fordham. Allow me to present myself. I am Alexander, the ninth Duke of Fordham."

The gentleman's face went grave. "I had not heard about the late duke's death. He was such a young man. A most grievous occurrence, to be sure. I am very sorry."

"Thank you." Alex waited a moment before broaching the matter at hand. "Would you be Mr. Christie?"

"I am. How can I be of assistance to you?"

"I understand my brother recently purchased a Rafael?"

"That is correct."

"For a most significant sum."

Mr. Christie's head inclined. "It brought far more than any of us expected."

"I daresay there were some disappointed bidders."

"When the bidding got to such heights, all of them dropped out, save Lord Garth."

"Poor fellow. Did he seem terribly disappointed?"

"He was. That evening. But next week a Rembrandt came on the market, and he was able to purchase it for significantly less. He told me it must have been Divine Providence that he was overbid on the Rafael because he always preferred Rembrandt over Rafael—and he saved rather a lot of money."

"I am happy to learn that," Alex said. "I had thought if the fellow was terribly upset, I'd offer to sell it to him, but as my brother really wanted the Rafael, I shall keep it."

Settled in his coach, Alex's thoughts turned to Georgiana. It had now been five days since he'd seen her. He would go to Hartworth House this morning for the twofold purpose of bringing her his copies of the *Edinburgh Review* and discussing suspects. He would share the knowledge conveyed to him by Gates, he'd tell her about the Rafael bidder, and he would inform her of Lord Barnstaple's suspicious behavior.

* * *

Georgiana was having serious difficulty sleeping. Each time she had snuffed her candle and climbed upon her bed, she began thinking about Fordham. During the day she kept so busy with Freddie's correspondence she had no time for idle thoughts. But once she was in bed, that rakish duke intruded on her thoughts likes weeds encroaching on a well-tended garden.

She did not want to think about him. She did not want to be another of his conquests. Most of all, she did not want to be attracted to him.

Lamentably, she was doing all those things.

Uncharacteristically, she was unable to control her own mind. Why did Fordham have to have such an effect upon her? No one else had ever disordered her thoughts as this man did. When she was with him, she felt as giddy as a school girl. When she was away from him, she longed to see him.

In the past five days she had not seen him, and she was going mad with want. Tonight was the fifth straight night she'd lain in her bed, her thoughts of him like tentacles filling every crevice in her brain.

Why was it that in so short a time, this man had come to know her as no one else ever had? There was between them an undeniably close connection.

It was impossible to steer her thoughts elsewhere. She could easily imagine him leading men into battle. He would have commanded their respect. She pictured him—his skin, his hair, the flecks in his mossy eyes—all tawny shades of gold. A smile inadvertently curled her lip as she recalled his strength. His powerful build united with his powerful personality to form this man who was her torment.

She was ashamed at how easily she had transferred her affections to the brother of her betrothed, and she was even more ashamed she had kissed said brother with more passion than she'd ever kissed her betrothed. All of this was so wrong. The laws of England forbade a woman from marrying the brother of her husband. Even though she was not wed to Freddie, she knew that Society would scorn her if she fell in love with his brother.

Then her thoughts turned dark. Would the soldiers who served under him still respect him if they thought him capable of killing his brother? Those suspicions bothered her significantly more than her own shame at being captivated by him. She did not want to think Fordham guilty of Freddie's murder. Her every instinct told her to trust him. This man possessed so many noble characteristics it was impossible to consider him guilty of murder. Or was it?

She thought of his sister admitting that their mother had feared either Freddie or Alex would kill the other. She thought of his *desperate* need for money before Freddie was killed. But she could not reconcile those two things with the man with whom she'd spent so much time the past few weeks, the man she had come to know, the man adored by his sister.

Which brought her back to the fact she had not seen him in five days. That she missed seeing him made her angry with herself.

Hour after dark hour she lay there beneath her blankets, listening to the wind upon her casements and the crackle of the dying fire in her grate, and all the while longing for Alex Haversham, the Duke of Fordham, like she'd never thought it possible to long for a man.

Would he come the next day? What should she wear? How should she act? Arrogant? Kindly? Welcoming? Her heartbeat roared when she thought about the possibility of being alone with him, of melding her body to his, of opening her mouth to his kisses.

Then, like a pendulum, those same thoughts of him repeated until dawn edged into her bedchamber and brought sleep.

* * *

Alex gathered up Philip Lewis's essays to take to Georgiana. It was a wonder he'd actually saved them. He normally did not allow piles of periodicals to accrue in his library. It didn't suit his tidy nature. But there was so much good, solid sense packed into those succinct literary works that he'd had difficulty tossing them. More than once he'd gone to those gems of wisdom to borrow snippets with which to enrich his own Parliamentary comments, and once he'd even quoted from one—an action which had inordinately pleased Harry Wycliff. Harry was responsible for introducing Alex to Lewis's writing.

As eagerly as Alex wanted to be with Georgiana he was aware that his long absence had earned the lady's ravishing smile when last he'd visited. *Keep her hungry.* That was his intent where Georgiana was concerned. Then he could hope to be rewarded with an enthusiastic welcome.

When he went to Hartworth House on the sixth day, he was met with a calamitous scene. A hysterical Lady Hartworth was prostrate on the settee in her downstairs bedchamber, clasping a letter in her hand. Her daughter, whose iron determination was the only thing keeping a rein on her own emotions, stood over her mother, holding a small vial of vinaigrette beneath her parent's nose.

His first thought was that the woman's soldier son had been killed. Though Alex felt an intruder, he wanted to be useful in a time of overwhelming grief. "What's happened? How may I be of assistance?"

Georgiana took a deep breath and spun toward him. "Mama's been notified that her four-year-old grandson has sustained a serious injury."

His brows lowered with concern. "I am at your service to convey you to Alsop."

The dowager gave a great sniff. "That is

exceedingly kind of your gr- gr- grace, though I don't know how I could be civil to the child's mother."

"You see, Mama blames—and not without cause—my sister-in-law for her overindulgence of the children."

"My little Huey was permitted to walk upon the roof of Alsop," Lady Hartworth interjected, then launched into another crying fit.

"At four years of age?" Alex asked, incredulous.

Georgiana's tear-brimmed eyes met his as she nodded. "It doesn't bear contemplation, but there you have it."

"Did . . . did the lad fall?" Alex finally asked.

"Yes," Georgiana replied, "and it would certainly have killed him were it not that he landed upon the under gardener. Poor Huey wished to see if he could fly like a bird."

Alex's breath swished from where it had been trapped in his lungs. "How fortunate that the under gardener was there."

Lady Hartworth drew another great sniff, daintily blew at her nose, then sat up to face Alex. "I cannot purge my mind of the terrifying thought of poor little Huey flying off that roof. I could happily strangle that half-wit mother of his."

"Such a reaction is most understandable," Alex said. "It does seem as though your grandson must have a guardian angel looking after him. What is the nature of his injuries?"

"My witless daughter-in-law did not say in her letter. She only assured me that he will be in a long recovery, but that his mental faculties—unlike his mother's—have not been impaired. I do believe Hester must have been dropped on the head when she was a babe."

"My sister-in-law did say that Huey has called for Mama."

To which Lady Hartworth launched into a fresh torrent of tears. "I should die if I were to lose my little hellion."

"I insist on looking after you ladies on the journey to Alsop."

"The Duke of Fordham's carriage is superior to ours . . ." Lady Hartworth said hopefully, eyeing her daughter.

The mother was obviously agreeable to his suggestion, but her unpredictable daughter could easily bristle at the notion. Holding his breath, he met Georgiana's gaze.

Georgiana's dark eyes met his, and she nodded.

"Would leaving in two hours be agreeable to you ladies, or should you prefer waiting until tomorrow morning?"

Georgiana looked at her mother.

"I can be ready in two hours, your majesty," Lady Hartworth said.

* * *

Once the duke's coach was weaving its way through the Capital's snarls of conveyances as it headed north, Mama launched into a tirade against Hester. "Such a terrifying accident would wield a massive change in any other person, but mark my words, that daughter-in-law of mine will continue allowing those children to do whatever they wish."

"Like jumping off roofs," Alex said.

The elder woman shuddered. "I cannot bear to think on it."

"Forgive me."

A moment later he asked, "What of your son, my lady? Will he not exert influence over his wife?"

Mother and daughter both harrumphed. "I love my brother, but he has an invisible defect. He lacks a spine."

Lady Hartworth nodded ruefully. "My late husband always said it was a pity Georgiana wasn't a male. She would have made a splendid marquess." The dowager lowered her lashes coyly and added, "Despite her great beauty and femininity, Georgiana *can* think for herself. My son has not a thought in his head that wasn't put there by someone else—usually that fool wife of his."

"Mama! Have I not previously told you *not* to praise me to the duke? If you continue to do so, I'll demand we return to Hartworth House and take our own coach to Alsop."

"See, your grace," Lady Hartworth said, "my daughter has spunk."

"Yes, I'm well aware of Lady Georgiana's . . . spunk." He grinned at the lady being discussed.

She tried to ignore the way she fluttered inside when he looked at her like that. "And," Georgiana continued speaking to her mother, "I'm not sure Hart actually listens to Hester. Upon his marriage he was told that the best way to get along with one's wife was to nod when she spoke, whether he listened or not."

"You may be right. Nevertheless, that moronic woman rules over him and the house," Lady Hartworth said.

Georgiana sighed. "She doesn't *rule.* She allows chaos to reign. Since Hester became marchioness, Alsop appears to have been decimated by a cyclone, but I will say the servants are devoted to her."

"Because she's a most lenient task master," Lady Hartworth said, despair in her tone.

Lady Hartworth harrumphed again. "One who requires nothing cannot be a master of anything."

"Enough lambasting of Hester." Georgiana directed her attention to the duke. "You will no doubt find Mama and me lacking in familial ties, but you will see for yourself when we reach Alsop. Now, your grace, tell me how far into the night you will allow your team to travel."

"Since the roads out of London are good and there's been no rain, I hope to travel for several hours."

She pulled back the blue velvet curtains to peer from the carriage window. Dusk was settling in. It would be completely dark in half an hour. This journey could be hard on her mother. "Mama, I know how fatigued you'll get. I'll just move across and sit by the duke while you stretch your legs out on our seat." Her mother was petite enough to be accommodated in such a manner.

"A very good plan. Thank you, my dearest."

Once Georgiana vacated the seat, she made a great fuss spreading the rug over her mother's lap and along her legs, tucking it under her mother's dainty feet.

Established on the seat next to the duke, Georgiana opened up her small valise and withdrew a neatly folded edition of the *Edinburgh Review*. "I thought I'd use the last of daylight to read one of Mr. Lewis's essays," she told the duke. "It was most kind of you to remember to bring them to me."

"You really are serious about educating yourself?"

"I don't like feeling inferior, and that's exactly

how I feel when I attend the Tuesday gatherings at Wycliff House. Your sister, Lady Slade, and Lady Wycliff make me look like an imbecile."

"You could never be an imbecile."

She expected her mother to concur with the duke and possibly launch into another bout of praise, but a glance across the carriage confirmed that her mother had already gone to sleep.

Georgiana immediately closed the periodical.

"You're not going to read it?" he asked.

"Later," she said in a whisper. "I know you have news of the investigation, and you must share it while Mama's asleep."

He nodded, and like her, spoke in a whisper. "My man first confirmed that Mrs. Langston could not perform on the night she received the news about Freddie's death. She sent word that it would have been impossible, given that she could not staunch the flow of her tears."

Oddly, Georgiana felt sorry for the actress. "And was your man able to learn anything from her servants?"

"He was most successful in getting the servants to take him completely in their confidence."

"And?"

"And they confirmed my convictions of her innocence. In the past year she's only left her house to appear on the stage, and her only male caller has been Sir Arthur—and me."

Her brows lowered. "So we know no more now than we did back at Gosingham."

"Oh, but we do. I have a suspect."

Her eyes widened. "One of the shooting party?"

He nodded.

"Oh, pray, do tell!"

He proceeded to tell her about Lord

Barnstaple's eagerness to acquire a section of Fordham property.

Relief flooded her. Surely this exonerated Freddie's successor. Lord Barnstaple must be the murderer! "That most certainly sounds promising. Now, how do we prove it?"

"We?" he asked

"Do not forget, your grace, it is I who first suspected Freddie's death was not from natural causes."

"And for that I am grateful, but it occurs to me if a man has killed once, he could easily kill again if he felt he were being threatened. It could be dangerous for you. I'll take over now."

"It could be equally dangerous for you." The fleeting thought that he, too, could be murdered was like an arrow to the heart. The memory of Freddie's dead body was all too fresh. She couldn't bear to see Alex's life snatched away too. *Alex.* This was the first time she'd thought of him by his Christian name. Of course, she would never call him by so intimate a name.

Nor could she ever unite herself to the brother of the man she almost married. It wouldn't be right.

"I've faced hundreds of soldiers intent on killing me, and I'm still here."

"I wish I'd never suspected Freddie was murdered."

"You'd want the real murder—someone we know—to be moving about without recrimination?"

She did not answer for a moment. "No, I don't suppose I would."

"Oh, I also went to Mr. Christie's."

"And?" Her brows elevated.

"No leads there. Freddie's biggest competitor in bidding found a painting he liked better the following week, so I don't believe he held a serious grudge against Freddie."

She nodded. "It was a rather far-fetched notion, but we couldn't ignore it."

The coach slowed. He lifted the curtain. "I believe we're stopping at the Lamb and Lion posting inn."

After the coachman bespoke chambers for the duke's party, they took a large, satisfying meal of roasted beef in Alex's parlor before retiring to their sleeping chambers. Georgiana shared a big corner room and a high tester bed with her mother.

It felt odd not having Angelique to help her ready for bed, but they had all agreed that bringing their personal servants and wardrobes would be too cumbersome and would delay their departure—a decision Lady Hartworth heartily endorsed.

It was the first night in almost a week that Georgiana readily went to sleep.

$\mathcal{C}$hapter 17

Were it not for her worries over Huey, Georgiana would have been deliriously happy the following day. She'd had the best night's sleep in a week. Though the day was unquestionably cool, the sunny blue skies completed her sense of well-being.

To please her Mama, who could not abide her daughter's propensity toward casual dress, Georgiana wore a traveling costume consisting of a long-sleeved, high-collared pale green cambric dress that was bordered in fancy needlework. This was topped with a Sardinian velvet Prussian Hussar cloak in a darker shade of green. Edged and lined with pink satin, the Hussar cloak featured a large hood. She carried a spotted ermine muff and wore half boots of soft green kid.

Despite that she refused to fall under Fordham's spell, she could not deny he was responsible for her good humor. Being with him gave her a comforting feeling, the feeling that nothing unpleasant could ever happen to her as long as she was with him. There was also a closeness between them like nothing she'd ever experienced. Were it not for the physical effect he had upon her, their connection was similar to what she'd felt with her youngest brother.

The knowledge that she was going to be spending the next several days so intimately connected to the Duke of Fordham helped to buoy her spirits during what would have been a most solemn journey.

Once they partook of breakfast and the duke procured a basket of food for later, they were on their way. In the carriage, she sat next to her mother, facing Fordham.

Her mother had brought along her lap desk, intending to write letters while they traveled. "Thankfully," Lady Hartworth said to the duke, "my recent affliction spared my right side. I don't know what I would do if I couldn't write my letters."

"Mama is a faithful correspondent." Georgiana helped her get situated, then announced, "I shall read all of Mr. Lewis's essays on today's drive." She reached into her bag to extract copies of the *Edinburgh Review.*

On seeing the publication, the dowager's brows lowered. "Your Papa had a most low opinion of the *Edinburgh Review.*"

"I promise I shall have an open mind," Georgiana said.

Lady Hartworth eyed the duke. "I realize, your grace, you have embraced the Whigs, and I assure you I hold no rancor toward you—even though the Fentons, like your Havershams, have always been Tories."

"That is most magnanimous of you, my lady," he said.

For the next few hours the ladies were occupied with their respective pursuits, but the duke just sat there. Most of the time he was peering from the window, but several times she looked up and found him watching her. She would immediately flick her gaze away. Was he studying her in his seductive manner, or was he merely interested in her reactions to Mr. Lewis's essays? She felt self-conscious and would have spoken sharply to him were it not for Mama, who was in possession of an inordinately inflated appreciation for high-born persons, especially dukes, and most especially this duke.

When afternoon came, Fordham obliged his coachman to stop. "I think we'll have a picnic here."

She admired his decision to stop here among the soft hills and dales. Georgiana nodded. "It will do us good to stretch our legs."

The dowager shook her head. "I refuse to use my cane on uneven terrain. I'm perfectly happy to stay in the warm carriage whilst you two go on."

Though Georgiana was wise to her mother's romantic manipulations, she also agreed that her mother was better off staying in the warm coach and not trying to walk on the uneven earth.

After assisting Georgiana from the carriage, the duke carried his rug along with the basket that held their picnic offerings. They walked some distance away from the coach, so far that they could no longer see it. The brittle grass was stripped of colour, and the occasional tree stripped of leaves, yet the austere setting offered a quiet beauty much to her liking. He found a spot in the sun at the crest of hill and spread out the rug.

They sat side by side, and she helped him unload the basket and spread out the food. "A nice assortment, I think," she said. There were hard-cooked eggs, apples, a loaf of bread, and a generous portion of local cheese.

As they were eating, he said, "I'm wondering if

you share your brother's traits. Like most Tories, he's unreceptive to other ways of thinking. I'm wondering if Mr. Lewis is succeeding in opening your mind to new ideas."

"I am not such a simpleton that I will toss out the old and adopt the new on the basis of one man's eloquent essays. Right now, I'm at the fact-gathering stage. Is it not to be desired to evaluate all sides before taking a stand?" She wasn't ready to admit it, but she agreed with every reform Mr. Lewis proposed, all of which made her feel like a traitor to generations of Fentons.

He spread cheese on a chunk of bread. "But you've spent a lifetime exposed to Tory philosophy—or lack of philosophy. What more could you possibly learn about them?"

"I resent that you accuse my family of lacking a political philosophy. Just because Hart's a blind follower doesn't mean that my father was. My father was a contributing Member of Parliament."

"Forgive me if I've disparaged your family," he said in a low, husky voice.

She had completely lost her appetite. All she could think of was his close proximity and the sincerity in his manly voice. She tried to suppress thoughts of their kiss because it stirred her in frightening ways.

"You read the essay about penal reform?" he asked, biting into his apple.

"Yes. It was brilliantly written. I could see how it influenced Lady Wycliff's talk."

"Do you agree with Mr. Lewis's proposals?"

"To disagree would be ludicrous, but you and I both know his ideas are merely idealistic dreams. It's nearly impossible to legislate such sweeping changes. Even if every man in Parliament agreed,

I doubt we could implement Mr. Lewis's suggestions in our lifetime."

"But you do agree that there needs to be a hierarchy of crimes commensurate with the punishments?"

"I do."

"I sense a *but* . . ."

She issued a soft giggle. "We really are coming to understand one another far too thoroughly." He more than she. No man had ever understood her before. "You're right. I was thinking of my Papa. I once tried to persuade him not to have a poacher arrested." She sighed. "He didn't listen to me. Later he told me that he was obliged to do things as they'd always been done. He abhorred change. So . . . your grace, I suppose you have been correct. I suppose the Tories resist change."

"You don't have to call me *your grace*, Georgiana."

Hearing her name on his lips underscored the closeness that had developed between them. For once, she did not correct him.

It did feel stiff to refer to him as *your grace*, especially in this setting. "I can hardly call you . . . Alex."

Their eyes met. "Oh, but you can, Georgiana, when it's just the two of us—as it's so often been."

Even though she'd come to think of him as Alex, she shook her head. It wouldn't do to invite such intimacy. She gazed off into the distance where a shimmering ribbon meandered through the landscape and caught her attention. "Look! A brook."

By then they had finished eating. "It will do us good to walk to it," he said.

Now that he was unencumbered of toting the

picnic basket and rug, he offered his arm, and they set off for the distant stream. The closer they came, the larger it appeared. As they crested the final hill, a wooden bridge came into view. It spanned the brook at its narrowest point, a distance of not more than ten feet. Hand rails were provided at either side.

The fierce wind here obliged her to pull her hood over her mussed hair and stinging ears. Mama would most definitely *not* like her hair getting disarranged.

As they stepped on the bridge he settled his hand at her waist. "I'm glad it's just you and me."

She was too, but she would not tell him so.

When he came to stop midway over the rushing water, she settled her elbows on the rail. She was content to watch the clear spring water flow beneath them, lulled by the sound of it. There was something so pure about country water. Being here made her understand men like Freddie and her brother who preferred the country over sooty London with its foul air and nasty streets.

A peace settled over her as she stood there on the weathered wooden bridge with Alex. His arm slipped around her. For that moment she felt one with him. It was if they were being absorbed by their tranquil surroundings.

She knew she should protest his intimate gesture, but she was powerless to do so. Such closeness seemed as natural as breathing. Her mind numbed with the pleasure of this moment. She did not want it to end.

He must have felt the same for they stood there, silent, for a great long while.

Finally, he turned to her so slowly it was as if he feared she would stop him. When she didn't, he drew her against his torso. Cradled into his muscled chest and encircled by his powerful arms, a feeling of femininity surged through her— and something more, something intense. Being in this spot in this man's arms was the only place on earth she wanted to be. Her face lifted as his lowered to meet for an excruciatingly tender kiss.

Her reaction to this kiss was even more powerful than before. For this time her opposition had been tossed to the wind and she clung to him, merged to him as if he were part of her.

For this moment in time she could forget that this man was a known rake. She could forget that this man was the brother of her recently deceased betrothed. But she could never forget the intoxicating joy of this moment.

After the kiss, his hands cupped her face as he stared into her eyes. She had never seen him like this. He conveyed a depth of emotion inconsistent with the tales of his inconstancy.

As their eyes locked, she thought of how much she did *not* want words to intrude on this . . . this whatever it was that made her feel as if she were drunk with happiness.

Then he spoiled this moment with words. "You and I are supremely compatible, Georgiana."

She could have wept. He spoke the absolute truth. She could never hope to find one such as he, one to whom she could become a single being. In every respect, this man appealed to her.

But it was wrong. She could never unite herself to the brother and heir of the man to whom she had been betrothed. Even though she had not actually married Freddie, she still felt honor bound to adhere to laws against mating with the brother of the man who would have been her husband.

Additionally, Alex had not even said he wished to make her his duchess. He had long avoided marrying the many women he bedded. To give him his due, he likely had not been in a financial position to offer marriage.

Now he was. Her heartbeat stampeded at the very notion that he might wish to wed her. She could weep.

It took a moment to compose herself for the deception. She smiled and tried to act flippant. "How can you say that when I am a Tory, your grace?" What a traitor she was! In every way. After being at the Tuesday morning gatherings, after reading Mr. Lewis's eloquent, perfectly logical essays, after being with Alex, it was impossible for her to agree with the Tories. A thorough transformation had come over her.

She and he *were* supremely compatible— something she could never acknowledge. She wouldn't even allow herself to call him Alex.

He looked wounded, and his voice was solemn when he spoke. "Alex."

She swallowed. Because of the ardor of their kiss, she would this once call him by his Christian name. "Alex." It sounded reverent. *I have to be strong.* She drew a deep breath and started to leave the bridge. *Their bridge.*

This time he did not offer his arm. "The reason you won't acknowledge what's between us," he said, "is that you feel guilty because you never kissed Freddie like you kiss me."

She refused to answer. The maddening man was always right! He knew her too thoroughly.

"Perhaps it *is* too soon after Freddie's death, but I'm a patient man. I'll have you, Georgiana."

She did not understand. *Have me?* Was he hell-bent on bedding her? Or was he determined to make her his wife? Not that it mattered. Either way, she must deny him.

Only to deny him was to deny herself.

* * *

Alex watched somberly as she prepared a plate of food for her mother even though Lady Hartworth showed no interest in eating.

"How was your picnic?" the dowager asked her daughter.

"It was lovely."

"You kept your hood on? It's beastly windy today. Glad I am that I stayed in the coach."

"Most of the time I kept it on."

Lady Hartworth shifted her gaze to him. "And how did you enjoy the picnic, your grace?"

"In some ways, it was the best I've ever experienced." He would tell no one of his grave disappointment when Georgiana destroyed his soaring happiness as thoroughly as flame to paper.

"I peered through the window but didn't see you," Lady Hartworth said. "You must have had the opportunity to stretch your legs rather a lot."

Did the lady guess that he'd wanted to be completely alone with Georgiana in order to make love to her? Was that the reason she didn't accompany them? From the mischievous glint in her eyes, Alex was almost certain of the dowager's encouragement. "It felt good to walk, and the landscape was much to my liking."

"We found a brook," Georgiana added.

The memory of its bridge and what occurred there was like twisting a knife in him. The way she had so eagerly clung to him throughout the tender kiss was as intoxicating as downing a flask of whisky. How could such joy have been so easily snuffed? His eyes met hers and she quickly looked away. But not before her cheeks flamed.

"My daughter adores walking—and she's an exceptional horsewoman. I understand your grace is exceedingly enamored of horses."

"That I am, my lady."

"Mama," Georgiana said in a warning voice, her brows lowered.

"Oh, I beg your pardon, dearest. I didn't mean to boast on you. I was merely stating a fact."

He eyed Georgiana, shrugging. "Much as if she stated that you're a very beautiful woman."

The colour hiked higher in Georgiana's cheeks.

"Exactly!" the dowager said.

Georgiana uttered something unrecognizable, seized her tapestry bag, and withdrew more copies of the *Edinburgh Review*. She continued reading these until darkness filled the carriage several hours later.

As the wheels churned and the dowager scribbled her letters, a hopelessness engulfed him. All the ground he'd gained with Georgiana had been lost. She was too headstrong to ever admit they were pulled to each other as if by some magnetic force.

He would be better off to drop her at Alsop and never have to see her again. For despite their undeniable attraction to one another, she had convinced herself that she preferred to exclude him from her life.

He would still have to endure two more torturing days in her presence. Then he would see her no more.

By the time they found an inn to stop at for the

night, rain had made progress almost impossible and had brought a biting chill. No amount of coverings could render the carriage comfortable.

They were all grateful for the warm parlor where they took their simple meal, yet throughout dinner a coolness had settled over the gathering that made easy conversation impossible. "I would talk politics," he said, "but as you are so staunch a Tory, Lady Georgiana, I have little to say." With that, he stood, moved to the fireplace, and stood warming himself until the ladies took their leave.

* * *

Mama went to sleep quickly, but Georgiana was incapable of sleeping. All her joy of the previous night had been stripped away, and she had only herself to blame. Throughout the long night with rain beating upon the casements, hardly a moment dragged by that she did not dwell on being held in Alex's arms, did not remember the bliss of their kiss. She had no experience to measure against such short-lived happiness. Even as she had been experiencing such unbridled joy, she had prayed that words wouldn't destroy it.

Then he had to speak, and his words leveled her back to propriety. Alex was her forbidden fruit. To the depths of her soul, she regretted that she must deny him.

As dawn crept into her chamber, she came to the heartbreaking realization that she would die a spinster. For she would never be able to love any man save Alex, and loving him would bring shame to both their families.

When they left the inn the next morning, the rain had stopped, but the muddy roads would restrict their progress. She had read every word in every copy of the *Edinburgh Review* so now she borrowed her mother's lap desk and began to pen letters—anything to keep from having to speak to Alex.

Sensing her stiffness toward the duke, Lady Hartworth attempted to engage him in conversation. He was polite but noncommunicative. The ensuing silence was almost unbearable. Hour after hour the only sounds were the rattling of the coach wheels and pounding of horse hooves.

Then as night came, a calamity befell them.

Chapter 18

Only the exterior coach lamps prevented them from being in the total darkness that had come so quickly. As the coachman had lighted the lamps, Alex gave instructions that they were to stop at the first inn they came to. "Where in the devil are we?"

"We be between Palding and Grantham, yer grace."

Alex sighed. That meant they'd be at Alsop— barring a nasty storm—by early tomorrow afternoon.

The rain had ceased, but the muddy roads made the ride decidedly uncomfortable. And Georgiana's silence had made the journey intolerable. Thank God they'd reach Alsop tomorrow.

Not long after they'd stopped to light the lanterns, the silence of the barren countryside was interrupted by the pounding of hooves quickly followed by shouts from the coachman. Alex bolted upright. "What the devil?" He slung back the curtains to peer from the window.

Panic sliced through him. Four masked highwaymen, each wearing a wide-brimmed black hat, were bearing down on his coach. Alex would have brought armed outriders and postilions had he any inkling highwaymen still lurked on this road. It had been years since he'd heard of a robbery here.

He watched in terror as one of the highwaymen leapt from his horse to mount one of Alex's team. He wasn't afraid for himself. He'd faced far worse in the Peninsula. But if they saw how lovely Georgiana was, they might want more than her jewels. . .

How cursed cruel it was that he had nothing more than his bare hands with which to defend the woman he had come to love.

His carriage lurched to a stop. Alex snatched his coin purse and tossed enough coins for tonight's lodgings to Lady Hartworth. "Hide these."

She stuffed them into the bodice of her dress.

Then with one last look at a terrified Georgiana, he threw open the door. If he stayed in the coach, it would be impossible to defend the ladies. He had to get on his feet. Perhaps then he could parry. In a fair fight Alex was considered to be a fine pugilist, quick of feet and fist, but this would in no way be a fair fight. Still, he had to try.

He jumped from the carriage and slammed the door. A quick scan confirmed that the vile man who'd stopped his team now held a sword to the coachman's throat, and another man with a black cloth obscuring his face and a musket aimed at Alex had dismounted and was closing in on the coach while two more accomplices remained on horseback, their muskets trained on Alex.

"Here," Alex said, procuring his coin purse. "You may have all my money." He tossed it to the man who stood in front of him. The jingling sound of the nearly full purse should appease them. The crest on the carriage identified him as a duke, and even the lowest born knew how wealthy dukes were.

To Alex's surprise, it was not the man on foot who spoke, but one of the horsemen. Was he the gang's leader? "We want the women's jewels, too."

How did they know he was traveling with women? They must have been following at a discreet distance for several hours. Had they been at last night's inn? Alex wanted to threaten to kill them if they so much as touched the women, but an unarmed man against four armed men had nothing with which to threaten or to bargain.

He continued blocking the coach door with his body, even knowing such a ploy was foolish.

"Move, or he'll kill ye," the mounted leader said. Was the man who stood a foot from Alex mute?

His hands balling into fists, Alex heaved a sigh and moved. He stood where he could still look into the carriage when the assailant opened the door. If the man hurt Georgiana in any way, Alex was prepared to fight him off—even if it meant dying.

The man on foot, who was an inch or two taller than Alex, rushed past him and threw the door open. He said but a single word. "Out."

So he can talk.

"But my mother's an invalid," Georgiana protested. She stripped off a sapphire ring and offered it to him. "Take this. It's all I've got with me."

The masked man snatched it.

Lady Hartford removed pearl earrings and pendant and a ruby ring and held them out to the man, who greedily took them.

Alex detested his own helplessness. He vowed to never again travel without a weapon. He chided himself for not at least bringing Gates. His valet had more than proven himself to be exceptionally capable with either musket or sword.

The almost-mute man brushed past Alex and tossed the jewels to the leader. Unconsciously, Alex noted the horse beside him—the horse of the man on the ground. There was something familiar about the horse.

From out of the blue, Alex cried out in pain. It felt as if his skull had been halved. Blood streamed from his head. He spun around to face the man who had attacked him. The man on foot aimed the bloodied butt of his musket at Alex again. Alex's vision clouded, but he was cognizant enough to lunge at his attacker and ram a fist into his masked face.

The man fell back, cursing. Then he sturdied himself and turned the gun around until the barrel pointed at Alex. Alex's heartbeat drummed madly. He was not quick enough to prevent the foul man's finger from pressing the trigger and firing.

It felt as if Alex's chest had exploded.

The last thing he remembered as he dropped to the ground was the whorl on the riderless horse's hide.

* * *

"Alex!" Georgiana shrieked as she flew from the carriage. She was aware that the man who'd taken her jewels—the man who'd shot Alex—was mounting his horse, but even if he'd held a gun on her, she would have bolted from the coach. All she cared about was Alex, whose bloodied body lay crumpled on the muddy earth.

Was he dead?

Her heartbeat pounding out of her chest, her hands trembling, she hurled herself to kneel beside him. Great rivulets of tears flowed, obscuring her vision. Even though drawing her own breath was a struggle, she wanted to determine if he still breathed but didn't know how to do so. She'd thought to place her hand over his heart to see if it beat, but the front of his shirt was puddled with his blood. She recoiled. This couldn't be happening! Minutes ago, he was teasing her. Now he showed no signs of life. It was worse than the most grotesque nightmare. *God, please let him be alive.*

She leaned into him, her tears slickening his bloodied cheek as she placed her face close to his mouth. Her breath stilled as she tried to determine if he were breathing. Several seconds passed, and she still could not tell.

In the meantime, the fourth highwayman had left the coach's box, mounted his horse, and ridden away, freeing the coachman to come to her assistance. He leapt down, his landing splashing mud everywhere, scurried to her, and spoke in a somber voice. "Is the master dead?"

There was anguish in her voice when she answered. "I don't know."

"Allow me, my lady." He came to squat beside Alex's lifeless form, lifted his employer's wrist, and placed his fingers upon it in an attempt to feel his pulse.

Her very breath trapped in her lungs as she waited for him to either verify that Alex had died— or give her the best news of her life.

By now her mother had managed to climb from the coach unassisted. She had removed her cloak and came to place it over Alex's wound. "We must sop up the blood. The important thing is to minimize the loss of blood."

Mama would not believe him dead!

Georgina somberly watched the coachman as

she fervently prayed for Alex's life to be spared. It wasn't just that she . . . loved him. He was put on this earth to do good. He had to live!

Finally, a smile seeped across Prine's bearded face. "I feel his pulse."

"Thank God," Georgiana and her mother said at once.

At that point, her mother took charge. "My grandfather was a surgeon, and each summer when I stayed with them, I would accompany him on his calls. I know a thing or two about musket wounds."

Georgiana was astonished. She herself could barely view the massive amounts of lost blood and not spew and swoon—yet her frail mother was going about the business of removing Alex's bloody shirt and attempting to stop the flow of blood. It was a side to her mother she'd never before seen. It was difficult to believe this was the same woman who had always been exceedingly coddled by her late father.

"Mama, I beg of you . . . do not let him die," Georgiana whimpered.

"I most certainly will not allow my future son-in-law to die."

"He hasn't offered for me."

"He means to."

* * *

Her mother tended to Alex's wounds—he also had sustained a head wound—and wrapped his head and bare torso with strips of a clean shift taken from her valise. Prine and Georgiana lifted Alex into the carriage for what turned out to be a short ride to the closest inn, The Roost. Preferring to suffer the cold herself rather than inflict another hardship on this man fighting for his very life, Georgiana wrapped him in her Sardinian velvet Prussian Hussar cloak for the journey.

Despite that Georgiana held his hand and murmured to him throughout the ride, Alex did not gain consciousness—which made her feel woefully low. Not only was she sick with worry that he wouldn't survive, but she was also ashamed that her mother and not she had ministered to him in the life-and-death situation. Georgiana was apologetically useless in a sick room. She'd never been able to tolerate the sight of blood.

The porter at the inn assisted Prine in carrying Alex to the inn's best room where they laid him upon the large tester bed. "Quick!" Georgiana commanded the porter. "We must have a fire to warm the chamber."

Instructions had already been given to summon a surgeon to remove the musketball.

The porter set about lighting a fire, and each minute thereafter the flames increased.

Within a half hour a doctor much the same age as Alex came. When he saw how the linen wrapped his torso, he commended Lady Hartworth. "That's the very thing. Unfortunately, I shall have to remove it in order to remove the musket ball."

Lady Hartworth moved to Georgiana. "Go sit down by the fire and don't look at what the surgeon does. We don't need you keeling over. One cracked skull is all I can tolerate."

Her mother sensed that Georgiana would not have been able to leave the chamber where the man she loved held on so precariously to life.

Whilst the surgeon worked on Alex, Georgiana was aware that he was doing things to his patient that would previously have had her hitting the floor in a dead faint. When the surgeon near Alsop put stitches in her younger brother's head after he had fallen from a tree, she had lost consciousness. But, oddly, tonight she was too frightened for Alex's welfare to be sick herself.

The sweetest sound she'd ever heard was when Alex moaned in pain. It was the first noise emanating from him since the musket felled him. Her pleasure was tempered with sympathy. She did not want him to suffer.

"You are giving him laudanum?" she asked.

"Most certainly, my lady. And I will leave a store of it with you. He'll be needing it."

After the surgeon removed the musket ball and closed the hole, he turned his attention to Alex's head. Holding her breath, she looked away when he began to unwrap the bloodied strips of linen from Alex's head.

"Should you like for me to procure more linen strips?" she asked.

"That would be most helpful," the surgeon said. "These are saturated with blood."

How peculiar that she could hear *blood* discussed without becoming woozy. She went to the room next door, which had been allotted to her and her mother, and retrieved her own linen shift, which she proceeded to tear into strips.

When she gave the strips to the surgeon, she avoided looking at Alex.

"A few stitches are all that's needed here," the surgeon proclaimed, "The wound's not deep." When he finished he said, "I shall come to check on his grace at midday tomorrow. I don't think the head wound's anything serious, but I'd like to check a few things when he's conscious. Feel free to summon me if there's need."

"We are most indebted to you," the dowager said.

The surgeon found the dowager. "By the way, my name's Ferrers. I hadn't wanted to take needed attention away from the patient for introductions. I understand the patient's a duke?"

"Yes. He's the Duke of Fordham. I am Lady Hartworth, and this is my daughter, Lady Georgiana Fenton."

Georgiana curtsied. "We are very grateful you came to us, Mr. Ferrers." She moved to him. "Will he . . ."

"He should make a full recovery—barring infection, which is always a concern. No vital organs were impaired."

"What do we need to look for?" Georgiana asked.

His face went grim. "Fever, but I think it's too soon for that. If infection should set in, it probably won't do so until he's showing symptoms of recovery."

"I pray there's no need to see you before noon," Georgiana said solemnly as he left the chamber.

One look at her mother told Georgiana that the ordeal of the past two hours had greatly fatigued the convalescing woman. "You need nourishment and rest, Mama. Oblige me by going to our chamber. I promise I'll fetch you if there's any regression in the duke's condition."

Even Lady Hartworth's eyelids were drooping. "Very well. You'll stay with him throughout the night?"

Tears brimming her eyes, Georgiana nodded. "I couldn't bear to leave him."

Her mother patted her shoulder. "I know, my

love. I know. I've asked that a tray be sent to you."

Georgiana shook her head adamantly. "Eating would be impossible."

Left alone with his eerily still body, Georgiana was unable to remove her gaze from him for fear of some catastrophe. How helpless he looked as he lay there, his head wrapped. At least the linen was now free of bloodstains. At the base of his skull, little tufts of his golden hair poked out from beneath the bandage. Her gaze shifted to his closed eyes. The lashes matched the golden tufts. All that he'd been through that night had not altered his fine looks.

She studied his face. For an instant she remembered standing there staring at Freddie's face after he died. If this man who looked so much like Freddie died, she did not believe she would want to continue living.

The rise and fall of his chest made her feel less melancholy. She prayed her thanks that Alex was alive and continued to beseech the Almighty to preserve his life.

Though he was unconscious, she felt compelled to communicate with him, even if it was just by touch. She took his hand and threaded her fingers through his, faintly squeezing. "You are not alone, my dear Alex," she murmured. "You will be surrounded by those who care about you. I vow I will do everything in my power to see that you fully recover."

He did not respond.

For several hours she stood at the side of his bed, holding his hand and murmuring endearments to him. She regretted that she had not acknowledged her love for him. She regretted it profoundly if her rejection of him had caused

him any melancholy. She vowed that if he
recovered she would do anything in her power to
make him happy. He *had* desired the deepest
physical intimacy with her. If he recovered, she
vowed to give herself to him—even if he chose not
to offer marriage. Even if Society scorned her.

For Georgina's love for this man was more
powerful than a surging tide.

Even though there was a chair by the bed, it
was so much lower than the bed she wouldn't
have been able to clearly see his face in the soft
candlelight. So she stood until exhaustion
overtook her in the early hours of the morning,
then she went to the other side of the bed and
climbed on top it, stretching out beside the
invalid. Comforted by his light snore, she went to
sleep.

* * *

The surgeon returned an hour before noon.
Georgiana had just returned to her chamber to
change her clothing while her mother sat at Alex's
bedside, but when Georgiana heard the surgeon,
she hurried back, even though her hair had not
been dressed.

"No, he hasn't regained consciousness," Lady
Hartworth told the surgeon as Georgiana strolled
into the chamber.

"That's not unheard of with these head
wounds. Laudanum, too, will promote deep sleep,"
the surgeon said. He lifted the covering. "I'll just
redress the bandage around his chest. Blood's
been oozing through it."

A wave of nausea crashed over Georgiana, but
she managed not to swoon.

"Would it be safe to move him?" Lady
Hartworth asked.

The surgeon paused, pursing his lips. "I would definitely advise against it. Not on these muddy roads. It would be best to wait until the wounds heal and the roads dry."

Awakening to sunshine had helped lift Georgiana's spirits—that and the fact Alex had made it through the night.

After the surgeon left, Georgian addressed her mother. "Prine can take you on to Alsop. You could be there long before dark. I know you want to be with Huey. Prine can be back in the evening to be here with me until Fordham's well enough to travel."

"I don't like leaving you—an unmarried maiden—alone here with a man at` death's door. If he were in dire need, you'd likely faint dead away!"

"I think the gravity of his injuries pulled my thoughts away from spilling—either myself or the contents of my stomach."

Her mother looked pensive. "I do believe you may be right."

"And you mustn't think of me as a helpless maiden. I am four and twenty. Do not forget, the surgeon will be at my beck and call."

Lady Hartworth sighed. "I do need to be with my precious Huey. And I do need to send Prine back with more money with which to pay for the extended stay at the inn and to pay the surgeon. Such a nice man."

When her mother left the chamber, Georgiana took her place beside the bed. She placed her hand on Alex's forehead. "No fever. That's good." Then she pressed his hand within hers and spoke tenderly. "Good morning, Alex."

Her hopes for a response were dashed.

$\mathcal{C}$hapter 19

The next several days would have been intolerable for Georgiana without Prine's assistance. He was not only a devoted servant, but he was also genuinely attached to his master and helped Georgiana in innumerable ways. He would hold Alex up while she coaxed him to swallow laudanum. He would see to it that meals were brought to her and tea brought for the duke. He changed the duke's clothing each day.

In one way, though, she would not accept his help: she would not allow him to spell her at the sickbed. Though she trusted the man, there was an exceedingly slim chance that he might have been Freddie's murderer, on account of his young son's accidental shooting death.

Georgiana could not bring herself to leave Alex's side. When she needed sleep, she'd taken to climbing upon the bed beside him. Hang her reputation! She cared not for anything except Alex and his recovery.

It occurred to her that Alex would want his closest friends to know of his current situation, so with tears streaming down her cheeks, she penned a letter to Lord Slade—to share with Lord Wycliff—apprising him of the duke's injuries.

The surgeon came each morning and evening, and each night she lay beside Alex, mournful of his recovery and yearning for his touch. In three days she had seen almost no progress, save a slight reduction in instances of his moaning from pain. She had to console herself with that.

But such consolation came without hope. Hour by hour she held his hand and stroked his face and whispered sweetly. During those long, discouraging days, she clung to her memories of the times they had spent together and regretted her coolness that had kept them apart. How she wished to have back those moments!

On the night of the fourth day she stood over him, cupping his face with a gentle hand. "Oh, my dearest Alex, how I wish I had told you that I'd come to love you. I was too proud and too foolish." She sighed. "I'd never experienced such potent feelings for any man. You knew that. You knew me better than I knew myself."

* * *

Through the fuzzy, cloudy disarray of his mind he was vaguely aware of a throbbing head and searing pain in his abdomen. But most of all, he felt the presence of an angel. And roses. This angel comforted him with soothing tones and words of love. As he came more fully into consciousness, he realized his angel was Georgiana—not the Georgiana who'd so heartlessly rejected him. This Georgiana called him *Alex*. This Georgiana said, "I wish I'd told you how much I'd come to love you."

He wanted to tell her he was in love with her, too, but he couldn't seem to climb from the stupor of his lethargy, couldn't seem to open his eyes. He lay there for a considerable period of time before the cobwebs in his brain cleared. In spite of his pain and discomfort, the knowledge that Georgiana loved him gave him a bubbling sense of contentment.

She no longer held his hand, but he knew she was close. Then it occurred to him she was on his bed, beside him. His eyes came fully open. "Georgiana," he said, but his weak voice was almost unrecognizable.

He rolled to his left. It hurt like the devil to move, but he was rewarded with the vision of her lying beside him, fully clothed in that white dress with the purple ribbands.

She smiled as her hand came up to cup his face. Her great dark eyes looked incredibly solemn as she spoke with concern. "Thank God you've awakened. How do you feel?"

"Like I've been shot from a cannon."

To his surprise, she did not sit up but continued lying beside him, nodding and stroking him—first his face, then his arm, then the back of his hand. Had a doxy done it, it would have been brazen. But when Georgiana stroked him in such a manner, it still reminded him of an angel. "Do you remember sustaining your wounds at the hands of those highwaymen?" she asked in an uncharacteristically gentle voice.

He groaned. "It's starting to come back." He remembered the man on foot bashing his head. Then the last thing he remembered was that same man shooting him with a musket. He'd thought he was being killed. "How did I live through it?"

"The surgeon said no vital organs were struck."

"And you? They didn't . . . try to harm you or your mother?" His heartbeat pounded.

"No. They left as soon as you fell."

He nodded. "It seems I'm indebted to them."

Her mouth gaped open and the tenderness in her voice was gone. "Whatever for?"

He gave her a sly smile. "For making you realize you love me."

There was a mischievous glint in her eyes when she said, "You odious man!"

"Had I the strength, I'd compromise you right now, you beautiful vixen."

Her lashes lowered seductively, and she whispered. "And I'd let you, my darling."

It seemed impossible that a man with such grave wounds could feel such astonishing happiness. "Of course, you will be my duchess."

"I had thought it wrong to want to marry you because you were Freddie's brother. After all, it's against the law to marry your deceased husband's brother. . ."

Even though it hurt him to move any part of his body, he reached out to touch her hair. "That law only applies to widows. Do you not remember a few years back when the Duke of Bedford died suddenly and his heir married the lady who'd been betrothed to his brother? She was the daughter of the Duke of Gordon. I assure you, they've been accepted everywhere."

"Oh, yes! The Duchess of Gordon's daughter! I'd forgotten. I was still in the schoolroom when it happened."

Her solemnity had fled like the shedding of a winter coat. She sat up. "You must eat."

He shook his head. "I have no appetite."

"Perhaps just some soup? Or what about porridge?"

He saw that it was dark outside. "I'll eat in the morning. I can see you're going to be an overbearing mistress to my recovery."

"Indeed I am."

Those were the last words he heard before he

slipped back into sleep.

* * *

When the doctor arrived the following morning, Alex was sitting up in bed allowing Georgiana to spoon porridge into his mouth—only because it hurt like the devil for him to move his arm to feed himself. He was rather afraid the significant row of stitches in his belly would unravel. "Ah, Ferrers, my future wife tells me you've given me the best of care, and for that I am sincerely grateful."

Ferrers looked from Alex to Georgiana, then broke into a broad smile. "Allow me to say, your grace, it is most gratifying to see you sitting up and talking. I'd begun to fear that injury to your head was more serious than I'd at first thought."

"I feared the same," Georgiana confessed in a somber voice.

"If his grace hasn't dispelled your fears, my lady, I most sincerely will. The patient appears to have made a remarkable recovery."

"So now, sir," Alex said, "you must tell me when I can leave this place."

Georgiana rolled her eyes. "He is lost without his valet."

Eyes glittering, Alex eyed her. "As are you without your maid, my dear. Your hair is a disaster."

"His grace is noted for his honesty—even when it's ungallantly directed at me."

"Allow me to say I do not find your hair a disaster, my lady," the surgeon said. "But to return to the duke's question, I think it best to wait until the stitches are removed." He went to the bed.

"And when will that be?" Alex asked.

"They cannot come out until the skin has

grown together."

Alex frowned. "How many days, typically?"

"Typically, two weeks."

"And I've been here?"

Georgiana answered. "This is your fifth day."

"I daresay I could remove them myself," Alex said. "It wouldn't be the first time."

"I did notice your grace had a number of scars on your upper torso," the surgeon said.

"The duke was a Peninsular officer until last year," Georgiana explained.

"So that explains your tough constitution." The surgeon went to lift away the sheets. "May I have a look?"

Alex nodded.

Ferrers went about rebandaging the wound. "You're healing well, but I'd advise continued bed rest until the wound closes better." He then turned his attention to Alex's wrapped head. "Since this wound was much shallower, I daresay we should be able to leave off these wrappings from your head." He proceeded to unwind the linen. "I shall attempt to clean away the dried blood, since Lady Hartworth told me her daughter is prone to fainting at the sight of blood—though I will say your injuries do seem to have toughened the lady. She's been a most competent nurse."

Alex's eyes met Georgiana's, and they shared a tender smile.

Once the surgeon left, Georgiana sat in the chair beside his bed. "Don't tire yourself by sitting up for too long."

"I confess it feels good *not* to be lying down." He proceeded to ask her a bevy of questions. Where were they? How far were they from Alsop? Had she heard of her nephew's condition?

"Mama wrote to say Huey's out of bed now and confined to an invalid's chair while his broken leg and broken arm heal. She's decidedly thrilled he shows no signs of impaired thinking – which I will own, she feared, given the lad's mother's mental deficiencies!"

"Was your mother overly wrought over the loss of her jewels?"

Georgiana shrugged. "My mother's first concern was you. Her ministrations on your behalf more than made up for my embarrassing revulsion to blood. Her grandfather was a surgeon, and she had learned a great deal from accompanying him on his rounds. *And* she's in possession of the added bonus of being able to witness blood without swooning."

"I'm very grateful to her."

"As eager as she was to get to Huey, she would never have left you had it not been that Ferrers was so good about coming. As the world knows, I am as useless as a bottomless bucket in a sick room."

"I beg to differ. It's the rare gem of a nurse who never leaves her patient."

Tears welled in her eyes and she spoke haltingly through threatening tears. "I thought as long as I was there, you couldn't dare die."

"Of course I couldn't die. Not before I had the satisfaction of proving I was right in my assessment of your . . . desire for me."

"I declare, if you weren't so infirm, I'd throw something at you."

"Your mother would disown you if you once again injured me. I still have a scar on my face from your little temper display, *my beloved*."

"You really are too odious, *dearest*."

They smiled at one another.

"Tell me if your pain worsens, and I'll give you laudanum."

He shook his head. "I won't have any more of it. I saw too many wounded men in the Peninsula sacrificing their effectiveness in battle whilst in the grip of the demon laudanum."

She nodded.

"I've been thinking about the robbery on the road. Did anything strike you about it? Anything odd?"

"Of course. I saw no reason for the man to shoot you. It wasn't as if you hadn't fully cooperated. He couldn't have known about the few coins you held back with Mama."

"I agree. Not only the shooting, but also the vicious ramming of the butt of his musket into my skull. It was such a mean thing to do, it made it seem as if he wanted me . . . dead."

Their eyes locked. She swallowed. "The Fordham curse."

"Yes, I suppose that's what I'm thinking. I haven't heard of highwaymen on that road in years. It's almost as if these men were there to kill me, and the robbery merely a means of covering up their true motive."

"You must be right! That would explain why the man who shot you said but one word. He didn't want us to hear his genteel voice."

"By Jove! I believe you're right. I knew there was something niggling at my memory. That must have been it. It's likely we might know my attacker. With the darkness, the huge black hats, and the masks obscuring their faces, it would have been impossible to identify any of them."

"Oh, Alex," she said, her voice forlorn, "I would

so much rather it have been a run-of-the-mill robbery. This is so much more mortifying. Someone means to kill you."

His mouth tightened. "Next time I'll surprise him. I'll have the upper hand."

"It must be your cousin. If you died, he'd become a duke."

"He's not like that."

"Is he exceedingly wealthy?"

"What does that signify?" The sitting up and taxing his brain were depleting the little bit of energy he possessed.

"He might kill for the wealth of a ducal fortune."

He shook his head. "I beg you not malign my cousin. I'm sure he could never commit murder, and besides my attacker was taller than me. Robert's shorter."

"I'm happy to know that. But who?"

"I wish to God I knew." His gaze darted to the door. "Do me the goodness of summoning Prine."

She simply obeyed without questioning him.

A moment later the coachman entered the sick room.

"Ah, my good man, allow me to say how grateful I am for your excellent care. Tell me, you have a musket stashed under your seat, do you not?"

"I do."

"Will you allow me to have it?"

"Of course, your grace."

Alex might be in a fragile state, but he needed to be able to defend himself and the woman he loved.

After Prine brought the musket, Alex sank down to a reclining position, his eyelids lowering.

"Oh, my dearest, I've tired you excessively.

Please rest. We can discuss this later."

* * *

He dreamed about horses. One horse, to be precise. Oddly, this horse was in front of Georgiana's house in Cavendish Square. It was a beauty. Chestnut with white stockings. Great head. Sixteen hands. What made this beast even more memorable was its whorl. Right on its withers. The magnificence of the beast was even more remarkable given that it was the property of that pompous piece of baggage that dressed himself like a colour blind fop, Lord Hickington.

When Alex awakened, the room was in darkness. He sat up and faced Georgiana.

"Hungry?" she asked in a tender voice. "It's time for dinner."

"As a matter of fact, I'm ravenous." This was the first time post shooting he'd felt like eating. It must be a sign that he was on the road to recovery.

As he watched her glide from the chamber, a deep sense of heady possession rushed over him. How fortunate he was to have won the lady's affection. How fortunate he would be to claim her as his wife. Were it not for the fact someone was desperate to kill him, he would be the most fortunate man in the three kingdoms.

Gloom was settling over him when she returned a few minutes later. "Our meals will be brought up shortly," she said. "I'm so happy you're finally able to eat."

He barely listened. He was trying mightily to remember something, something about that night the vile man in black tried to kill him. Something significant, he was certain. For some reason, his recent dream and the actions of that night were intrinsically tied together.

"When the food comes, do you fancy me feeding you?" she asked.

He shook his head. "I'm tired of being treated like a bloody invalid."

She gave a little giggle. "But you are an invalid!"

He laughed too. "Right you are. Again. But I can still be tired of it."

"It's only been two days since you've regained consciousness. I can see you're going to be a most difficult patient."

When the food came, she placed a tray in front of him. Then she put her own tray on the table near the fireplace, drew a side chair up to it, and returned to cut up his mutton. "I believe we should try to minimize the repetitive actions that might aggravate your stitches."

He was powerless not to watch her with surging pleasure. How he loved this woman! When she returned to her table, he looked at the musket that was propped against the wall beside his bed. It was comforting to know that if he had to, he could protect this woman he loved more fiercely than he'd ever thought possible.

They ate in silence. With each chew, his thoughts swirled around the whorl on Hickington's horse.

Then he remembered. It was like sunshine bursting through a blackened sky. Only there was nothing sunny about this. As Alex had fallen to the ground that night, clutching his bloodied chest, he'd noticed the whorl on the gunman's horse. Hickington's horse.

"I know who killed my brother."

$\mathcal{C}$hapter 20

Her eyes widened. "How can you possibly know such a thing?"

"Because I know horses better than a mother knows her offspring."

"Whatever can you be talking about?'

He explained about the whorl on Hickington's horse. "And as the murderer shot me that night, the last thing I remember seeing was the whorl on the fine beast. In the exact same spot where it was on Hickington's horse. An impossible coincidence."

"You're saying Lord Hickington's the man who tried to kill you?"

He nodded. "The same man who murdered my brother."

"But why?"

"Need you ask?"

She did not respond for a moment. "You can't really think the man would kill in order to obtain my hand in marriage? I told you there's nothing that could ever persuade me to wed that man."

"You may know it, but he obviously doesn't." Now that Alex thought about it, he recalled some talk at White's about Hickington owing Lord Landsdowne money—money he'd not been able to repay. "As lovely and desirable as you are, my dearest, you have one more attraction that Lord Hickington no doubt wants to get his hands upon."

"My dowry!"

"Twenty thousand, is it not?"

She nodded solemnly.

He stuffed the last of his mutton into his mouth and threw off his covers.

"Pray, what do you think you're doing?" she demanded.

"I've got to go to London."

She leapt from her chair and came to stand in front of him. "You most certainly will not! You're not fit for traveling."

"My dear woman, I've ridden horses over rocky terrain with injuries as bad as this."

"But then you didn't have to worry about leaving a heartbroken lover should you die."

He tossed a mischievous glance at her, his eyes glittering. "I wouldn't be so certain about that."

"You odious man."

He nodded. "I know, you could throw something at me were I not nearly mortally injured."

"You're a mad man if you can even contemplate exposing yourself to such brutal rigors of travel in the condition you're in."

"You have little understanding of a soldier's constitution." He went to push past her.

She eyed his boots in the corner, raced to them, and plunked herself down on top of them.

"What the devil do you think you're doing?" he demanded.

"You'll not be going without your boots, and I'm not moving."

"You'd have me possibly reinjure myself lifting you?"

"You'd dare not!"

A loud rap banged at his chamber door. Their puzzled gazes met. "Come in," he said.

In strode Sinjin and Wycliff.

"What the devil?" Alex said.

Georgiana sprang to her feet. "Thank God you've come. This deranged man is trying to go to London tonight. The surgeon has said it wouldn't do for him to attempt travel before next week."

Sinjin's gaze centered on Alex's chest. "Look at you! You've bled through your shirt."

She shrieked and came to him. "Please, allow me to look at your wound."

"What?" Alex said. "And have you swooning and possibly injuring yourself."

Wycliff strode to them. "Back to bed, old fellow. I'll have a look."

Alex reluctantly agreed. "How did you know I was here?" he asked.

"Lady Georgiana wrote us," Wycliff said.

Sinjin nodded. "We came right away."

"From the lady's letter, we feared we might not be in time."

She shrugged. "I was rather worried."

With great tenderness, Wycliff removed his shirt. "You've literally made a bloody mess. Whatever possessed you to think you were in good enough condition to travel to London?"

"I've learned who killed Freddie—and who tried to kill me."

Wycliff stopped mid-action, his mouth gaping open. "Who in the bloody hell?"

"Lord Hickington."

"And his motive?" Sinjin asked.

"He wished to unite himself with the fair Lady Georgiana Fenton—and her twenty thousand."

Wycliff shook his head. "And you learned this

how?"

Alex explained about the whorl on Hickington's horse.

Sinjin shrugged. "I will own, no one knows horse flesh like you, and if you say that's Hickington's horse, then it has to be."

Wycliff proceeded to remove the bloody wrapping from Alex's midsection while Georgiana brought fresh linen with which to bind him. "Would you look at all those stitches!" Wycliff exclaimed. "And you were idiot enough to think you could make the trip to London. That wound on your head must have impaired your thinking."

"How is the head wound?" Sinjin asked.

"It's already healed," Alex answered. "By the way," Alex said, striving for casualness in his demeanor, "you must offer Lady Georgiana and me felicitations."

Wycliff stopped dead in his actions, whirling around to face Georgiana just as Sinjin was saying, "Lady Slade and I knew at once you two were perfect for each other. We are both very happy to wish you many years of domestic bliss."

"As do I," Wycliff said. "I can want nothing more for my great friend than to wish him as happy with his wife as I am with mine." He then turned from Georgiana to Alex. "You have demonstrated excellent judgment in one matter, it seems. A pity you would jeopardize your life just when you've found the perfect mate."

After he finished bandaging and dressing Alex, he said, "In the morning Sinjin and I will return to London. We'll get the magistrate and go to Hickington House to arrest the blackguard. Rest assured with the three of us all members of the House of Lords, we'll be in a position to ensure our colleagues in that chamber convict him of Freddie's murder."

* * *

It was three days later when Sinjin, Wycliff and the magistrate went to Hickington's House on Piccadilly to arrest him. They rapped at the door, which was in need of fresh paint. His footman answered. "Lord Hickington is not in London," the servant said.

Wycliff wondered if this was a ploy used by the servants when addressing those to whom Hickington owed money. There was one way to find out.

Walking some little distance away from the house, he said, "We shall just go around to the mews. Someone there will know if Hickington was going on a journey."

Hickington's extraordinary horse was there as was a groom. "Where is Lord Hickington's carriage?" Sinjin asked.

"His lordship sold it 'bout a year back. Just this morning he hired a coach for a journey he's taking."

Wycliff and Sinjin exchanged questioning glances. "Did he say where he was going?" Sinjin asked.

The groom shook his head. "He just said he'd be gone four or five days."

Good Lord! Had the murderer learned that Alex was still alive? Did he mean to go back and kill him?

* * *

It must be a sign that Alex's condition was improving when his inability to get comfortable interfered with his sleep. It must also be a sign that his stitches needed to come out when they started to itch so badly he wanted to tear off his bandages and have a go at them right in the middle of the night. He might have done so were it not for his concern over awakening Georgiana.

There was also the fact she would not look favorably upon such an action by him. Her didacticism might have been trying were it not an indication of how thoroughly she loved him. It still felt as if he'd won life's sweepstakes to have captured her heart. That knowledge made him feel as if he'd grown a foot taller.

He lay there wondering if it would hurt his wound were he to scratch with gloved hands. Better yet, he ought just to yank out those blasted stitches!

A noise near his window caused him to still and listen more carefully. It was impossible to see anything because his room was totally black. He tried not to breathe as his ears perked. The noise was barely discernible, but it had to be a gradual raising of the sash.

His heartbeat raced. Someone was trying to enter his bedchamber even though it was on the second story. Was it Hickington? It had to be.

The musket! Alex went to sit up but fell back when the mattress creaked.

There was the unmistakable sound of a foot hitting the floor by the window. The thumping in Alex's chest grew louder. He lunged toward the side of his bed to grab the musket, but the pillow was yanked from behind his head.

He means to smother me as he did Freddie. Alex had no intentions of calling out, for to do so would jeopardize Georgiana. In this darkness, Alex hoped Hickington would never know she was lying beside him. The man likely had a weapon.

Just as the pillow was being shoved into his face, Alex used all his might to heave Hickington away.

Taken by surprise, the attacker gasped harshly.

It was enough to awaken Georgiana. "What's going on?" she asked, panic in her voice.

By now the two men were engaged in fisticuffs. "It's Hickington," Alex managed. "Get out of here!"

She leapt from the bed. He could tell from her footsteps on the wooden floors that she was not going to the door. "Get the hell out of here, Georgiana!" he shouted.

Hickington punched him in the gut. Alex cried out in searing pain.

"Leave his grace alone, or I'll shoot," she said into the darkness. She must have snatched the musket. He'd wager she had no idea how to use it.

Alex spun away and lunged toward her, but he fell short.

"Now I'll have to kill both of you," the intruder sneered. The voice was unmistakably Hickington's. Next a volley of fleet fists pounded into Alex's abdomen. He cried out in excruciating pain. When he fell to the ground, the pummeling continued. Alex fought like a healthy twenty-year-old—even though his stitches ripped.

Then there was the deafening sound of a musket being fired, the smell of gunpowder.

Alex held his breath.

The pounding stopped. Then there was a thud as Hickington fell to the floor.

$\mathcal{C}$hapter 21

London, three weeks later

A quiet wedding was in order. The Duke of Fordham's name had saturated every newspaper in the country. Could there be a soul left who hadn't read that in defense of his life, the duke had killed the murdering Lord Hickington?

So on this, the most momentous day of his life, Alex shared with just his two closest friends, his cousin Robert, and his unmarried sisters. His beloved bride had even fewer guests—only her mother and little Huey.

Unable to choose between Sinjin and Wycliff to stand up with him at the front of St. George's, he chose both. Always, it had been the three of them sharing everything. Since their marriages, Alex had felt left out, not because he'd been replaced in their affections by their wives but because both his friends had achieved a perfect union, and it was something he longed for. He'd never thought to find a woman who could bring him the happiness his friends had found with the wives they so adored.

In all but one respect, he had found his perfect duchess in Georgiana. He regretted that she aligned herself with the Tories, but he believed she would open her mind to the reforms he and the lords from Eton were working toward.

As he stood there clasping her hand and saying

his wedding vows to the only woman he could ever love, he felt another's presence: Freddie. He felt almost as if he could turn and touch him. It was as if his brother were giving him his blessings. He could almost hear Freddie say, *"You two are perfect for each other, you lucky dog."* A deep contentment took root in him and swelled. He looked down into Georgiana's lovely face and was nearly overcome with emotion.

After the ceremony the attendees gathered in the church's vestibule as rain pounded against the tall timber doors. Huey limped up to the bridal couple, leaning on a thick cane. "Lookey, Auntie G! Grandmama permitted me to cut down her cane and use it—as long as I don't hit my sister with it."

Georgiana whirled to her Mother. "You aren't using your cane anymore?"

Lady Hartworth shrugged. "No need. In fact, when we return to Hartworth House for the wedding breakfast, you'll find that my bedchamber's been moved back upstairs. It's my wedding gift to you. I've fully recovered, and you needn't worry about me anymore."

Mother and daughter embraced.

Alex wondered if Lady Hartworth's stroke had been fate. The lady's long convalescence was what kept Georgiana from marrying Freddie. Alex was becoming a firm believer in fate.

Prine came to collect the bridal couple, offering a large umbrella. Once they were in the carriage, Alex tenderly kissed his wife. When he went to put his arms around her, she stiffened and pulled away. "You, my dearest husband, know very well that every time you try to embrace me, it aggravates your wound."

"But, my dearest wife, it's such an enjoyable way to hurt."

They laughed.

That was something else he loved about her. She and he frequently laughed. She could laugh at herself, and she could admit when she was wrong, excellent qualities to have in one's life partner.

She snuggled closer to him, on his good side. "My darling, I have a confession."

His heartbeat thumped. "Pray, do not tell me you're already wed to someone else."

Her dark eyes flashing, she shook her head and frowned. "As much as I've insisted that my sympathies are Tory, I have to admit that I have no sympathies for the Tories. I've become as passionate over Whig causes as those ladies at the Tuesday gatherings."

"I would say that's the best wedding present I could have asked for." He *had* married his perfect mate.

They rode for some little distance in utter contentment. "Do you know," he said, "I think you realized very early on that I was smitten with you. I think you might even have believed I was falling in love with you."

"I might have."

"But it occurs to me that I've never articulated it. So, on this our wedding day, I want you to be perfectly clear on the matter. I *did* fall in love with you very early on. I love you more than I ever thought it possible to love a woman." He stopped and drew a deep breath. "Whew! I hope I don't have to do that again. I'm not terribly good at such confessions. Lack of experience, I suppose."

He and his duchess laughed together. He could

see that theirs was going to be very close to a perfect marriage.

The End

The Lords of Eton series

This book is the third in my *Lords of Eton* series about three aristocratic lads who were best friends at Eton and how their escapades and interests continue to tie them--and the women they love--together after Eton.

The first book in the series is *The Portrait of Lady Wycliff*, which is loosely based on my out-of-print book, *The Earl's Bargain*.

The second book in the series, *The Earl, the Vow and the Plain Jane*, is loosely based on my out-of-print book *His Lordship's Vow*.

Author's Biography

A former journalist and English teacher, Cheryl Bolen sold her first book to Harlequin Historical in 1997. That book, *A Duke Deceived*, was a finalist for the Holt Medallion for Best First Book, and it netted her the title Notable New Author. Since then she has published more than 20 books with Kensington/Zebra, Love Inspired Historical and was Montlake launch author for Kindle Serials. As an independent author, she has broken into the top 5 on the *New York Times* and top 20 on the *USA Today* best-seller lists.

Her 2005 book *One Golden Ring* won the Holt Medallion for Best Historical, and her 2011 gothic historical *My Lord Wicked* was awarded Best Historical in the International Digital Awards, the same year one of her Christmas novellas was chosen as Best Historical Novella by Hearts Through History. Her books have been finalists for other awards, including the Daphne du Maurier, and have been translated into eight languages.

She invites readers to www.CherylBolen.com, or her blog, www.cherylsregencyramblings.wordpress.co or Facebook at https://www.facebook.com/pages/Cheryl-Bolen-Books/146842652076424.